D A T E	D U E	

November Ever After

November Ever After

LAURA TORRES

Holiday House · New York

Library of Congress Cataloging-in-Publication Data
Torres, Laura.
November ever after / Laura Torres.—1st ed.
p.   cm.
SUMMARY: In the aftermath of her mother's death, sixteen-year-old
Amy finds solace in the company of her best friend, Sara, but then
she is shocked to discover that Sara is romantically involved
with another girl and has kept it a secret from her.
ISBN 0-8234-1464-7
I. Title.
PZ7.T64565 No 1999
[Fic]—dc21   99-17697
CIP

Chapter 1

IT WAS THE KIND OF MORNING made for catching frogs. Sara and I were long past the age to do this sort of thing, but it was our ritual, something we had done the day before school started for six years, and plenty of times in between.

We snuck out of Sara's basement. We never left from my house, although after my mom died, it wouldn't have made any difference. My dad slept heavy and even if he woke up for some reason, it would never occur to him to check my room. Mom would have. That's just the kind of person she was. She would have *known*, in the middle of the night, if I was gone.

Even so, we only snuck out when I slept over at Sara's house. Habit, I guess. This time, Dorothy,

Sara's mom, finally collapsed in front of the TV at about four-thirty in the morning. Sara went upstairs and put out her mom's cigarette while I went into the garage and got the waders. Dorothy's last husband was a fly fisherman, and when he disappeared, he left behind a trunk full of different-size rods, vests, hats, waders, and some other stuff we couldn't identify. We pulled the waders on, way too big, almost to our armpits, but perfect for frogging. We each clipped a piece of fishing line, tied back our hair with it, and stuck on a cap. Both of us had longish, medium-brown hair, mine wavy and Sara's straight. Sara had gold highlights put in her hair once a month, which made her light brown eyes seem amber. The fishing line never held a ponytail and usually ended up so tangled in our hair we'd have to cut it out, but we always did it this way. Sara tossed me the flashlight, and we slipped through the garage's back window.

The best time for catching frogs was actually around six this time of year, just as it was getting light, but the football team had an early morning practice and we didn't want to get caught. The pond was at the junior high school, separating the far athletic fields from the woods. The long skinny pond and the tall trees and thick vegetation— mostly ferns and moss and old logs covered with fungus—on the other side of the water created a natural barrier, but someone had put up a seven-foot-tall chain-link fence to keep the students and the baseballs in. One thing I loved about living just on the outskirts of Seattle was the mix of city and woods with not much in between.

It was pretty cold for September, so we walked quickly on the back path through the woods. I carried our white bucket, which used to hold that sickening-sweet-grocery-store-bakery-frosting. When the bucket was dry, if you put your nose near it and breathed deeply, you could still smell the sugary frosting in the back of your throat. You'd think six years of frogging would have erased any trace of sweetness.

We got to the edge of the fields and climbed over a slippery log to the pond. The chain-link fence cut the pond in two. Sara climbed the fence and dropped into the water on the other side, spraying me with the mucky water.

"You scared all the frogs away," I said, wiping mud off my nose.

"Only for a second. They'll be back. Stupidest frogs around," she said.

"How would you know? You've been catching frogs somewhere else?" I climbed the fence and went over the top carefully.

"Of course not. No one else would understand this," Sara said.

"Not true," I said, and slogged over next to Sara. "I know several eight-year-old boys who would get it."

"So we're strange," she said. "So what?"

"Only you," I said.

"If I'm not mistaken, the first time we came out here was your idea."

It might have been. Last May we argued for two days over whether it was Sara or me who kissed Billy Adams in the old cook shed behind the school playground in the second grade. We were both positive it was the other person. Finally, Sara just asked him straight out during trigonometry class. He sat directly ahead of us. His face turned red to the tips of his ears and he clammed up and wouldn't say.

"It was the second grade, Billy, it's okay to talk about it," Sara said. "We're just trying to settle an argument, not make you reenact the moment."

Billy looked over at me and I puckered my lips. Sara snickered and that did it. He turned around and held his head so straight for the rest of class he probably got a crick in his neck. So that mystery remained unsolved.

We both stood still and quiet, so the frogs would come back. When we heard the first croaking sounds, about three feet ahead, I lowered the bucket and turned on the flashlight. Sara moved forward slowly. We had done this so many times before, we didn't have to talk to each other to communicate. Once Sara and I practiced synchronized swimming for a whole summer, thinking our telepathic communication skills would make us perfect. But we never could stop laughing at the dopey nose plugs or hold our breaths long enough to get any good at it.

Sara grabbed a frog and threw it into the bucket in one motion. She didn't like to touch them for long. I shone the light on the frog. It held still except for its white throat, which expanded and deflated rapidly. Its front feet were both spread out so far it looked as if the transparent skin between the webbed toes was stretched so thin it would tear.

"It's a tiny one," I told Sara.

"No kidding. It was a lot faster than I expected. I almost lost it." She plunged her hands into the water and then dropped another frog into the bucket. We traded back and forth until the bottom of the bucket was full of green and brown frogs crawling all over one another and looking pretty uncomfortable.

"I'll let them out," I said, and started climbing back over the fence. We always let them go on the opposite side so we wouldn't catch the same ones over again. Just as I cleared the top, I heard voices coming from the path in the woods. Sara heard them, too.

"Jump!" she said, which I did, accidentally catching the bucket on the fence and sending frogs flying in all directions. I scrambled out of the pond and behind a big moss-covered tree. Sara had gone to climb the fence, but the voices were coming too quickly for her to make it over. She looked for somewhere to hide, but there was nothing but pond and flat fields on that side of the fence.

"Oh, please, oh, please, oh, please," I whispered. It would be too embarrassing to get caught. Someone saw us the first year we did this, when we were ten, and everyone called us "the frog girls" for an entire year. It's one thing to be known for catching frogs when you're ten, quite another when you're sixteen. I wished I couldn't see Sara so clearly. Hadn't it been dark just a minute ago?

The figures approached and Sara dove into the shallow pond water and stayed under until three boys carrying football equipment had cleared the fence, hopped over the narrowest part of the water, and walked off onto the fields. Luckily, they moved quickly. Sara came out sputtering, spitting, and swearing. I walked to the fence and shone the flashlight on her.

"You've got pond scum in your hair," I said.

She looked at me and raised her hand. In it was the biggest, fattest frog ever caught at the Northshore Junior High School pond.

"It's going to be an interesting year," Sara predicted as she set the frog free.

Chapter 2

I LEFT SARA SHIVERING by the pond and ran to her house. She couldn't walk back freezing cold and with waders full of water, so I'd have to borrow Dorothy's car and come get her. I crawled back into the house through the window we left open, hoping none of the neighbors was up getting ready for work. The morning light grew brighter by the second, and I felt like a freak running around in my waders without Sara. The waders kept threatening to slide off. I'd lost a lot of weight off my already-skinny body lately. Not on purpose—I just forgot to eat most of the time. I held on to the waders and thought about how things always seemed less ridiculous when Sara was with me. And how would I explain myself if Dorothy woke up?

I went up half a flight of stairs to the little Peg-Board where Dorothy kept extra keys to the car, but they weren't there. I knew Sara's house about as well as my own, but didn't know where keys would be if they weren't here. I headed up the stairs to look in the junk drawer in the kitchen. Tiptoeing past Dorothy, I noticed her purse by the chair. It seemed worth a look. I laid on my belly and dragged the purse toward me. It was open, overflowing with tissues. I gave the purse a little shake and heard the jangle of keys. I stuck my hand inside and my finger went into a tube of lipstick without a cap. Dorothy groaned and turned on her side in the chair, so her face was directly above my head. Her mascara was all smeared under her eyes and the bright red lipstick she always wore, even when she was sick in bed, radiated into the small wrinkles around her mouth. The best thing to do, I decided, would be to take the whole purse.

When I got downstairs with it, I dumped it out and searched through all the stuff. I picked up a scrunched white envelope with my phone number written on it and smoothed it out. Besides my number, it had my dad's office address written down, along with his office hours and phone number. My dad is the pastor of the church in town, and Dorothy has never set foot in it, as far as I knew.

Once when I'd talked religion with her, she'd cut me off with a wave of her hand, saying, "To each their own."

I turned the envelope over. "Anita Moore, 555-3452," was written on the back. Anita belonged to the cheerleading squad at school. I never paid her much attention until she started hanging around Sara last year, and this year she was like flypaper on Sara. Why Sara chose Anita for a friend is beyond me. It's not like I can't handle Sara having other friends. She's got plenty of them at school, but Anita bugs me. She's always looking at me funny. Like she wishes I would get lost. Obviously if Anita thought she was going to replace me as Sara's best friend, she didn't understand me and Sara.

I studied the envelope for a long time, looking for clues that weren't there, then crumpled it back up and put it in the purse along with all the other stuff except the keys, which I dropped in my shirt pocket. I returned the purse to its place before I left, in case Dorothy happened to wake up. Mostly, I didn't want her to know I'd been snooping.

I had planned to change quickly before I went back, but I'd taken too much time, so I ducked low as I ran to the car in full daylight.

Sara was waiting by the sidewalk on the edge of the school property where it was heavily wooded, her hair all tangles and hanging in strings. She looked more miserable and cold than mad, but she lit into me anyway.

"Where have you been?" she shouted as her teeth chattered. "I'm going to catch pneumonia!"

"I couldn't find the keys, so I had to steal your mom's purse and dump it out," I said, which made her stop yelling at me. "I found my dad's phone number and address written on an envelope in her purse," I said, leaving out the part about Anita's phone number. "What's that about?"

"Probably nothing," she said quickly. "She probably has the hots for him or something."

"You have to be kidding. My dad and your mom?" That scenario should have struck me as funny, but instead it hurt to think of anyone, especially someone who knew my mom, wanting a relationship with my dad.

"Like I said, it's probably nothing. Don't worry about it," Sara said. "Now get me home. I stink so bad I can't stand myself."

When we got back into the basement, Sara went upstairs to shower and I crawled back into my sleeping bag. It was seven-thirty, but Dorothy would let us sleep until at least noon, since she never stirred before then. I thought about how my mom would have known somehow that I was gone.

Once she said to me, "Amy, sometimes I can't tell the difference between me and you."

Most people thought she was overprotective of me, which was true to a certain extent, but she was so good and kind and loved me down to the soles of her shoes that I couldn't be too upset about it, even when it got downright annoying. Besides, it was nice knowing she was there for me.

Now, late at night I'd wake up sometimes and her voice would be clear as anything.

"You have a fever, Amy. I woke up all sweaty and knew you had a fever. You were practically glowing red when I came in here." Then I would feel the cool washcloth on my face and her soft hand caressing my cheek. Sometimes, in my sleep now, I even smelled her herbal shampoo-scented hair as she leaned over to kiss me.

I went to sleep, dreamless.

I drifted awake to pans banging around in the kitchen. I turned over to wake up Sara, but she wasn't there, although I knew she slept after her shower because her pillow was darker where the dampness of her hair soaked in.

"Amy! It's one o'clock!" Sara shouted from the stairs. "Come up and have some breakfast!"

My eyes were heavy and my head ached, like when you've slept too much, or taken a nap that lasted way too long.

Upstairs, Dorothy stood at the oven, scrambling eggs. She only makes two things well, a spicy sausage spaghetti sauce and scrambled eggs. She makes the eggs with buttermilk and cheese, and I could eat them for every meal. Sara says I wouldn't want them if that's all I ever got, like she did. Dorothy had on fresh lipstick and her bangs were hair sprayed the way she liked them, ratted and straight up to the ceiling.

Once my mom, who kept her own straight blond hair in a neat pageboy, said something to Dorothy about how much work it must be to fix her hair like that every morning.

"The higher the hair, the closer to God," Dorothy had said. My mom laughed. Another pastor's wife might have been offended, but Mom had a way about her that made everyone feel comfortable. Dorothy had never once said anything off-color in front of my mom. Mom had that effect on people—made them truly want to be respectful and good.

"Did you guys have fun sneaking out last night?" Dorothy asked.

I shot a look at Sara.

"What do you mean?" Sara asked, shrugging her shoulders at me.

"Last night. You girls think I don't know you've been sneaking out all this time?" She turned to face us.

Sara and I looked at each other, then we busted up laughing.

"What?" Dorothy asked, "What's so funny?"

That's the thing about Dorothy. Even though she knew we'd been sneaking out, she never bothered to stop us or even worry about it. The eggs started to sizzle and smell bad.

"The eggs are burning," I said. She whirled around.

"Oh . . . fuzzballs," she said, throwing the whole pan into the sink. She tried hard not to swear around me, although she slipped up more often than not. She turned on the cold water and jumped back as the hissing steam rose into her face.

"It's nothing to worry about," Sara said. "We're not getting into trouble or hanging out with weird people or anything."

"Just don't tell the pastor," said Dorothy as she scraped at the bottom of the frying pan. "He might think you're a bad influence on Amy." She pitched her cigarette into the sink with the burned pan. "And don't take my car again."

She turned around and looked at Sara, then me.

"Let's go out for pancakes," she said, and I tossed her the keys from my pocket.

Chapter 3

"**H**ERE'S THREE red-eyed, curly-winged flies,"
Sara said. She was peering in one of the small vials
of fruit flies in Ms. Newman's back room.

"I liked this experiment," I said. We'd done this
experiment together when we were freshmen. "The
red-eyed, curly-winged flies have both the recessive
traits, so they're the most rare, if I'm remembering
right."

"It must be, because all the rest of them look
brown-eyed," Sara said. "What's that disgusting
stuff in the vials with them?"

Each vial had a dirty yellow, waxy-looking cone
hanging inside from the top. The fruit flies swarmed
around it. "I think it's their food. It sure stinks."

"It makes me want to gag. You can't get away from the smell."

Sara and I were Ms. Newman's teacher's aides last year and again this year, since no one else wanted to do it. We got to work behind the counter of the science supply room, passing out creatures preserved in formaldehyde and earthworms to dissect. It was fun to freak out the freshmen, and if we noticed someone who looked gullible enough, we'd bring them in the back and show them the brain Ms. Newman kept in a big glass jar hidden under a towel. We would tell the kid it was the late Mr. Newman's brain. Usually the kid believed us, at least for a little while.

Really, the rows of jars with things floating in them and the weird chemical smells from the room were creepy, but Ms. Newman made it all worth it. All the other kids think Ms. Newman is a real crab, but Sara and I think she's the greatest. She drives an old-fashioned car and owns about twenty-nine cats. Sara and I were good students, and got A's in Ms. Newman's classes, even though she didn't pass them out like candy like the popular teachers did. She made us work.

After class Ms. Newman walked into the back room. We quickly threw the towel back over the

17

brain. We'd been trying to decide what to tell the freshmen this year.

"Can you girls stay after school today for a few minutes and help me get these class papers organized?" Ms. Newman asked.

I looked at Sara and she shrugged her shoulders.

"I guess," I said.

"Show a little enthusiasm," Ms. Newman said. "See you after school."

Organizing the class papers turned out to be a major feat. There were fifty-two pages to collate for the freshman science classes. Ms. Newman dropped off the stacks of papers and left because one of her cats was about to have kittens.

"Do either of you girls want one of the kittens when they're old enough?" she asked us.

I thought about what it would be like to have an animal around, something to take care of. Forget it. Dad and I can barely take care of ourselves. Sometimes neither one of us goes grocery shopping for so long we have to run to the mini-mart at the gas station at midnight to pick up a stale corn dog or a bag of chips to keep from starving through the night. How would we remember to feed a cat?

"I think you should take one, Amy," Sara said. "Your house is so quiet all the time. A pet would be a good thing."

"Sure, Amy," said Ms. Newman. "I'd love for you to have one of the kittens. It's not easy to find good homes."

"I haven't done the laundry in two weeks," I said. "You think I'd remember to clean out a litter box?"

"Good point," Sara said. "I'd take one but my mom's allergic."

Sara and I set each of the fifty-two piles of paper out on the L-shaped counter that went around the side and back wall of the room. We began collating them, each doing half at a time and then putting the two stacks together. After about twenty minutes, we both had paper cuts and didn't seem to be making any progress.

"I don't think I can stand this much longer," Sara said. "When is Ms. Newman coming back? How long does it take to have kittens, anyway?"

"I don't think she's coming," I said. "I didn't hear her say anything about coming back. Besides, she wouldn't leave newly born kittens to come here and do this. That's what she's got us for."

"Hey, look at this," Sara said. She was using a tool that looked like a little toilet plunger to pick up the papers. "This is better, but too slow," she said. "What else do they have in here?"

She rummaged around in the big drawer where they kept all kind of gizmos for who-knows-what.

"What do you think this is for?" She held up a thing that looked like a turkey baster.

"Let me see that," I said. I brought it over to the sink and ran water until the basin was half full. I squeezed the hollow rubber ball at the top of the baster thing so it filled with water. I squeezed it so the water squirted out and hit Sara, who was walking toward me, right in the belly.

"Sorry!" I said, though not convincingly because I was laughing.

"I cannot believe you just did that," she said and lunged forward to grab the baster out of my hand. I held it up high where she couldn't reach it and kept squeezing the ball, sending down a shower on both of us.

"Truce! All right! All right!" she screamed.

"Promise?" I asked.

"Promise," she said.

"What's the code? I won't believe you without the code!" I said.

"You can't be serious," she said.

"I'm serious!" I said, and squeezed again, sending water on top of her head. The code was a silly rhyme we'd made up when we were kids about the towns we were born in. I'm not sure how it came about, but it meant a promise that can't be broken, no matter what.

"Okay, okay, you win this time," she said. "Walla Walla, Yakima, onions and cherries, sis boom ba!" Then she held out two fingers for the snap. I bent my two fingers around hers and she pulled hers up while I pulled mine down, with exactly the same amount of force. It was something we'd perfected years ago, and no one else can do it. We used to show it off to everyone, until the time we got self-conscious about frogging. But we still used the code in private; it was like part of the fabric that made up me and her.

We collated the papers a while longer, but it was just too boring. So we started to make up games and think of different ways to get the job done. We'd been through about fifteen different ways by the time we tried the wheelbarrow method.

"Put all the stacks down on the floor," Sara said. We moved them to the floor in a straight row, making a turn at the bend in the L.

"Okay, now grab my ankles." She put her hands down on both sides of the papers and I lifted her ankles. It was hard because I was feeling light-headed from laughing so much.

"Go!" she shouted. I moved forward as Sara walked on her hands, picking up the first paper by putting her lips down on it and sucking it up like a vacuum, then letting go of the suction when we got over to the square wire basket on the floor. We made it through to about page 30, which took a good five minutes, before Sara's arms started to buckle.

"I can't do this anymore. Let's switch." She stood up quickly. This was a big mistake considering she'd been nearly hyperventilating and practically upside down for the last five minutes. She lost her balance and stumbled into the shelf that held all the bottles of weird things. The shelf shook and leaned in, all like it was in slow motion.

I ran over, even though it would be too late to stop anything from falling. At least I bent over Sara on the floor and let a heavy bottle hit my back instead of her head.

And then it happened. The brain jar slid from the shelf and hit the floor with a crack. It rolled across the floor, dribbling liquid along the way. When it smacked up against one of the stacks of papers, the cracked jar split in two and the brain slid over the top of the stack and came to a rest against the baseboard under the counter.

A stench that was like fingernail polish remover times a hundred with a dead fish thrown in filled the room.

We stayed still, Sara on the floor and me hunched over her, afraid to move. Then I noticed some tiny black bugs inches from my face.

"Fruit flies," I said.

"Shit," said Sara.

We still didn't move, unable to believe what we'd done. The fruit flies congregated around the brain and around our faces. It wasn't until one landed on my nose that I moved.

"We have to get this cleaned up," I said.

"There's more to it than cleaning up," Sara said, standing up. "What are we going to do with that?" She pointed to the brain. "I'm not touching it."

"I'm not either. There have got to be gloves or something . . ." I said, looking through some drawers. "Look, here's a trash bag."

"Good idea. Let's wrap it up and throw it away," Sara said.

"We can't throw it away. This was *somebody's.* We can't just get rid of it. If we can find an extra jar I could pick it up with this trash bag and put it in."

"What about the liquid? It'll dry out. We're going to be in trouble no matter what. We've ruined the brain. Let's just throw it away," Sara said.

"Well . . ." I stood there with the trash bag in my hand, wavering.

"What do you mean, well? You're supposed to know what to do. You always do the right thing. You're supposed to talk me out of throwing it away!"

"Why is it *my* responsibility to know what the right thing to do is?"

"Because you always know! That's the reason I hang around with you! You're my conscience!" Sara looked sincerely panicked, but like she was going to bust up laughing at the same moment. She was right, I usually did know what to do, until last November. Since then, I hadn't been able to make decisions or even tell up from down, let alone right from wrong. Besides, I'd never dealt with a brain and loose fruit flies before. It made me feel good, though, that Sara thought I was still capable of thinking straight.

"All right, here's the plan," I said. "You start putting back all the stuff that didn't break and I'll deal with the brain."

Sara put things back on the shelves and made choking noises if something gross got on her hands. I wrapped my hand in the trash bag and tried to get enough courage to pick up the brain. I finally just reached down and grabbed the thing. It was squishier than I thought it would be and it almost slipped out of my plastic-covered hand. I gagged a little bit as I flipped it through to the inside of the bag. I quickly tied a knot in the top of the bag. The fruit flies buzzed around as I soaked up the spilled liquid with a stack of paper towels. The papers the jar had landed against were soaked through.

"I think we can throw these away," I told Sara, "It's page 19, the periodic table. Isn't that in the textbook anyway?"

"Yes. It looks like only four vials of fruit flies got loose. Nothing else is completely broken here, just a few cracks in the jars and broken lids. I turned anything suspicious toward the wall. Do you think that's terrible?"

"Considering we're going to come clean about the brain, I don't think so," I said.

"What do you mean?"

"We are going to finish collating these papers and then we're going to Ms. Newman's house to give her this." I held out the trash bag.

"You're too good to be true," said Sara. "I hate you." She went over and opened the windows and we began collating the papers, minus page 19, as fast as we could.

Chapter 4

WHEN WE SHOWED UP on Ms. Newman's doorstep, she acted as if it was the most natural thing in the world.

"Come in, come in," she said. "We've got five new kitties! Come see!"

Any bravery I felt earlier about telling the truth evaporated. I concentrated on getting my breath back. Sara and I practically ran the two miles to her house.

"We have something to tell you," Sara said. She elbowed me and I held up the bag.

"What have you got there?" Ms. Newman asked me.

"It's . . . it's something from the back room." I choked on the words. Ms. Newman looked from me to Sara.

"It's that brain you kept in the big glass jar. We accidentally knocked it over, the jar broke, and so here it is," said Sara.

"We didn't know what to do with it," I said, my face pounding with embarrassment.

Ms. Newman's mouth opened and her eyes popped. She grabbed the bag out of my hand and undid the knot. When she opened the bag, that stench drifted out. I stared hard at the floor so I couldn't see her face when she looked in.

"Did you get the papers collated?" she asked, after a long silence. "I mean, when you weren't desecrating sheep brains?"

"Yes," Sara said. "We're real sorry about the brain." She looked over at me, smiled, and mouthed the words "sheep brain."

It did make me feel a little better, that it didn't belong to a human, but still, I really felt like an idiot here. When I'm with Sara, nothing seems strange or stupid, but sometimes, for instance right now, I felt like a cockroach caught in the corner of a kitchen by the beam of a flashlight. Out of context, out of order, and pitiful.

I'm not sure what Ms. Newman ever did with the brain. She set it outside on her back porch, never saying anything else about it. She didn't seem mad, which made it worse, somehow. It was like the time when I was little and was playing in my mom's walk-in closet, where I'd been told not to go. I opened a bottle of her best perfume, the one Dad gave her for their anniversary, and meant to put just a little on my wrist. I dumped the whole thing right there on her carpet. When Mom came in and found me, she just started crying. I wanted her to scream or yell at me or send me to my room, but instead she just knelt down there next to the spot on the carpet and cried. Her green eyes shone especially bright, rimmed with red from crying.

"It's okay, Mommy," I remember saying. "Daddy can get you some more."

"It's not the perfume," she said. She looked straight into my eyes, copies of her own green ones. "It's you."

That's probably the first time I felt mortified. I'd made my mother cry because I'd been bad.

I started to wail, and she hugged me tight.

"I'm sorry I'm bad," I said, and sobbed into her neck.

"You're not bad, Amy honey," she said. "Sometimes you just don't use your head. Next time you think harder before you do something like this."

"I promise, I promise," I said, and she ended up comforting me, the one who'd messed up.

I shook the memory out of my head and followed Ms. Newman to a closet. She opened the door and pulled the chain to turn on a dim bulb.

"Look how little they are," Sara whispered. We bent over the cardboard box, lined with a cushion, that held the mother and her five kittens. The kittens, their eyes shut and still wet-looking, slept in a pile inside the protective curve of their mother's body. Almost in unison, their small bodies heaved with their deep-sleep breathing. Something about them made my insides turn to mush and the pain I kept stuffed deep inside came to the surface.

During the day, although I'm always aware my mom is dead, I can go through the motions and keep the pain at a level where I can function. But every once in a while something random like these newborn kittens brings it out unexpectedly, filling my whole body, making my head spin and the weight of it crushing my lungs, my heart, and my spirit. When Sara's not with me, I feel so completely alone, I can't convince myself I'll get through this, that it will get better. I put my hand on her arm and leaned closer to get a better look at the kittens.

"Look at this one with the white spot around its nose," I said. All the other kittens were black, a few with white patches on a paw or their chest, but only this one had a spot on his face. The spot was the size of a pea, perfectly round and the kitten's nose sat right in the middle of it, making it look like it was all nose.

"The poor thing," Sara said. "I'll bet its brothers and sisters will call it 'Big Nose' or something. It hasn't got a chance." She looked at her watch. "Ms. Newman, can I use your phone?"

"Sure," Ms. Newman said. "It's right around the corner."

"Who are you calling?" I asked.

"Um, Dorothy," she said.

It wasn't true. Dorothy didn't care if she came home late. All I had to do was give Sara a look.

"And Anita," she added, coming clean. "I have to check the time for a study group."

I pushed Sara's lie to the back of my brain, because I figured she was protecting my feelings, that's all. I felt bad that Sara felt like she had to hide the fact she was friends with Anita. I'd make an effort to try and not make it so obvious I didn't like Anita. I didn't want Sara to have to sneak around in order to spare my feelings.

"Ms. Newman, can I have this one?" I asked, surprising me more than anyone. I held the kitten close to my face and touched his nose to mine. What was I thinking?

"Consider it yours," she said. "I'll bring it to school when it's old enough."

That night I lay in bed, unable to sleep again, watching the shifting shadows on my wall. The deep blue of the night turned to black and it closed all around me until I could feel it inside. The pain let loose in this blackness, the kind of pain that seemed like a cancer, invading every healthy thing left in me, slow but overwhelming. The kind of pain that is so deep I can't cry. This is what hell must feel like. I wondered if my dad felt this same thing, in his bed in the room next to mine. That my mother's death could cause this kind of depression and blackness and pain didn't surprise me, because it was just the opposite of everything she was to me when she was alive. It made sense in a way.

I floated awake the next morning, my guts still aching from last night. The sun on my face felt like my mother's hand stroking my cheek so many years ago. This was a memory I had forgotten I had, but it came clear now.

"You scared me, Amy," my mom had whispered. I must have been three or four years old. "I've never been so scared in all my existence. If I ever lost you, I'd curl up in a ball and die. There'd be nothing else to do."

She put her face to mine, her warm tears stinging my cheeks.

We'd been camping in Sequim, on the coast. There was a red tide that evening and we stood on the dock pitching rocks into the ocean, watching the splashes, like hot red sparks jumping off the water.

I sat on the edge of the dock over a deep pool and scooted forward to try and touch my feet to the water. I remember how the splinters felt going into my back as I slipped off the edge and fell into the water up to my chest, suspended by my bent-backward arms, throwing my chin forward, just above the water so I breathed in salt. I was too frightened to scream or cry or try to pull myself up. I simply hung on until my shoulders felt like they would pop out of their sockets. That's all I remember, really, until later that night when my mother whispered to me.

Now, I lay on my bed and let the wetness of my own tears warm in the sun on my cheeks. I didn't dare move, or the realness of the memory would disappear. I held on to this scrap of a physical sensation because it's all I had, all I would ever have.

Finally, I wiped my face dry and blew my nose. I hurried to get ready for school, anxious to meet Sara on the corner and forget about the night.

Chapter 5

"DO YOU THINK we're immature?" I asked Sara on the way to school. I tried to imagine anyone else in our class having an experience like we did yesterday afternoon.

"Immature? Hmmmm . . . No, I don't think so," she said. "I think we haven't lost our sense of humor, that's all."

We walked along, Sara humming a song I didn't know.

"Do you think I should try out for the musical?" she asked.

"If you want to," I said. Sara had an okay voice, but when she danced, she always drew a crowd.

"Well, it would mean a lot of hours after school and on weekends," she said. "I wouldn't be around too often."

"You worry about me too much," I said, although I felt a panic in my chest when she said this. Sara was the only person I wanted to be with, and being alone all the time was too awful. Everyone else just bugged me, or made me think about things I didn't want to think about or seemed insincere. I didn't want to be anybody's charity case. And I can never even relax around Dad, because since Mom died, we tiptoe around each other, careful not to talk too much about anything, in case we accidentally opened the wounds we carried, stitched with the thinnest thread.

Dad's thrown himself into his work, so he's not around too much anyway. After Mom died, the higher-ups asked him several times if he was sure he wanted to continue as pastor. He doesn't get paid much, it's a lot of work, and I guess they figured he was too emotionally fragile to have the burden of a whole congregation on his shoulders. Everyone knows a pastor is chosen partly on account of his wife, because she's like the mother of the congregation, and has to hold the family together because the pastor spends so much time away from home.

Plus, it's weird to have a single guy be the pastor, especially in a real family-oriented congregation. But he said yes, because he needed to be busy, needed to be serving his people.

When Mom died, all the ladies from church came to our house and tried to comfort me. Streams of them, for days on end, some I didn't even recognize. Their husbands stood out on the lawn with my dad, patting his shoulder and looking at the ground, or talked about the weather with him.

All of the ladies said the same thing, one variation or another of this: "Your mom was a special spirit, and God must have needed her in heaven. It was her time to go."

This never made me feel better. It made me mad. I needed my mother. It wasn't "her time." She died because a truck driver fell asleep and hit her head-on two blocks from our house. Was the driver supposed to be an angel, come to take her home?

One day, one of the ladies, Mrs. Bird, said, "Would you like me to help you fix your hair?"

I looked at her like she was from outer space, but she pulled a brush and some weird hairpin-looking things from her purse. As if it mattered what my hair looked like. As if it mattered that our house was clean. Someone was scrubbing out our refrigerator, cleaning crevices with an old toothbrush. Someone else had washed the kitchen floor on her hands and knees. My mother had never done either of these things. It was unnerving how people made themselves feel better by staying busy. I wanted to scream at them all.

Dad told me to be patient, that these people were motivated by love, and I should see it that way. While they didn't mean any harm, nothing they could do would fill up the crater in my heart when Mom died, so why even bother?

When Sara showed up, she told everyone to go home. Just cleared the room in thirty seconds flat. She herded the ladies right out the door.

"This is the worst thing that could ever happen to anybody," she said after they all left. "You must be mad as hell."

When she said that, I finally cried for real. Big, hysterical sobs that I thought would turn me inside out. She hugged me close and held me up and cried softly into my neck, absorbing some of my pain.

"Come on, I'll help you upstairs," she finally said. She guided me into my bedroom and got my favorite pair of pajamas, the soft flannel ones with pale blue flowers, out of the drawer. She pulled down the shades while I changed, big sobs still tearing out of me, and silent tears rolling down her cheeks. I climbed into bed, thinking I'd never get out.

"I'll be right back," she said. "I'm going down the hall for a second." She knew I'd fall to pieces if she left me just then.

She came back with a box of Kleenex, aspirin, a glass of water, my Walkman, and some of my favorite tapes.

"If it gets too bad, put on the headphones and turn up the music real loud so you can't think," she said. I nodded.

"I want to sleep, but I'm afraid to," I said.

"I'll sit here with you. Would that help?"

"Yes, I think so," I said. I shut my eyes tight and tried to squeeze out the pain, but it only got worse and I started sucking in gulps of air and crying that turning-inside-out kind of crying again.

I didn't have to pretend it was okay, because it wasn't, and it never, ever would be.

I stopped going to church, stopped trying to make myself feel better by thinking about heaven and angels and hope.

So after Sara said she wouldn't be around much if she was in the musical, I decided to be in it, too. I showed up in the auditorium for the tryouts after school on Wednesday, even though I can't sing or dance very well and the thought of being up on a stage gave me a major case of the willies. But I'd feel so lost without Sara, it seemed worth it. I grabbed a copy of the script and sat down in the back row, looking for a part that would be completely unobtrusive.

"Everyone! Everyone!" shouted Mrs. VanSickle over the noise. "Please, have a seat!" She reminded me of Ms. Frizzle in those *Magic School Bus* cartoons—freaky clothes and kinky red hair. The only difference was Mrs. VanSickle's dresses were cut so low in front and she was so tall, you couldn't look at her straight on without losing your train of thought, so most people stared at their shoes or up at the ceiling when they talked to her.

Peter Barnes, who I knew from church and who used to chase me every day at recess during the third grade, sat down next to me and jostled my elbow when he took off his backpack. His hair parted on one side of a big cowlick in his bangs and flopped over one eye. I dropped my script and it slid down the sloped floor underneath the seats out of sight.

"Sorry," he said. "Do you want mine? I'm just trying out for a chorus part, so I don't need it."

"No thanks," I said. "I'd better try out for the chorus, too."

"That's great. We'll be together. Sandra and the others are all trying out for the big parts," Peter said. He pushed the hair out of his eye. The others meant the kids from church. They operated as one big unit, so it didn't surprise me too much that although I'd never thought of Peter as the type to be in a play, he was here with them.

"I didn't know you were musical," he said.

"I'm not. Not really, anyway," I answered, realizing I must seem more out of place than him.

"Ah, Sara's talked you into this, right?"

"Actually, she doesn't know I'm here yet," I said. Peter didn't hear me because he was furiously waving at Sandra, who was up in the front row.

I was getting uncomfortable. I didn't want to have a conversation with Peter. I didn't want Sandra to have an excuse to come over and talk to me. Sandra and some of the other kids from church made themselves fixtures at my house every Monday afternoon after Mom died. They came to the door and invited themselves in and we all sat around and looked at each other. Sandra would start the conversation.

"How ya doin', Amy?" she'd say, all casual-like.

"Fine," I'd say.

Then we'd have stilted conversation for about twenty minutes, and they'd leave. I was "their project" and I knew it. I wondered if their parents made them come, or if Dad was behind it. He worries that I don't go to church anymore. But you can't force friendships. You can't make friends out of people who feel sorry for you. Gosh knows I feel sorry enough for myself.

It occurred to me that Peter never came those Monday afternoons. I'd see him around at school, and he'd smile at me or say hello, but he never seemed fake like the others. He was the only person from church that I didn't purposefully avoid. I'd gotten good at dodging around lockers and acting distracted to avoid eye contact, especially with Sandra.

"If you are trying out for the chorus, please follow Mr. Alberts to the gymnasium. Anyone trying out for a part, please stay seated," Mrs. VanSickle said.

Great. The only reason I came was to be with Sara, and now they're separating us? I wondered if the chorus would be separated through most of the practices. I thought about leaving, especially when I spotted Sara and Anita, the flypaper girl, next to her.

"Let's go," said Peter. He had a big, crooked grin on his face. That was something I'd always liked about him. "They want us to leave so we don't throw the real singers off key."

He put his hand on my arm and kind of led me through the crowd, which made me feel nervous, but I didn't pull my arm away because I liked how calm and sure he was.

Mr. Alberts led us through five songs and decided to keep us all in the chorus. I can't say that I sang very loud or very well because I couldn't concentrate on the music, only on Peter standing very close to me, singing and smiling. He smelled really good, like he just got out of the shower.

"Practices are Mondays and Wednesdays, three forty-five sharp," Mr. Alberts said. "Please pick up copies of the music by the door on your way out."

Peter stuck close by me as we left. The gym was hot and stuffy and I began to feel claustrophobic. The people who tried out for the main parts were filtering into the gym, too, and Peter was laughing and talking, with his hand on my arm again. I just wanted to get out.

I grabbed my papers without saying good-bye and darted through the crowd to the door and out into the cold, dark air where I could breathe. I finally found Sara back in the auditorium talking to Mrs. VanSickle. There was Anita, standing close to Sara and flipping her hair behind her shoulder and laughing. I couldn't believe it didn't annoy Sara as much as it annoyed me.

Sara raised her eyebrows when she saw me.

"I'm going to be in the chorus," I said.

"Well, congratulations all the way around then," Mrs. VanSickle said.

"Anita and I got the leads," said Sara as the three of us walked outside. Perfect, I thought.

"I knew you would," I told Sara. Maybe we could ditch Anita and walk home together, but she didn't seem to be going anywhere.

"Hey, can we give Amy a ride home?" Sara asked Anita.

"Sure thing," Anita said.

"What's with you?" Sara whispered to me on the way to the car.

"Nothing," I said.

"You're sulking."

"Am not." I tried to smile.

"Don't be jealous," Sara said. I stopped.

"Jealous? Of what? Of who?" I said.

"You're my best friend, you know," Sara said.

"Duh," I said, and rolled my eyes.

"Are you guys coming?" Anita said over her shoulder. Sara put her arm around my shoulder and gave me a quick hug, then we caught up with Anita.

We got into her red VW bug, which was full of pom-poms and books and clothes. There was no room in the backseat, so Sara and I squished into the front seat together. I told myself to relax. What was I worried about?

Anita dropped me off first, passing Sara's house on the way, and I went into the empty, dark house alone.

Chapter 6

THE NEXT DAY Sara met me at the corner as usual to walk to school. She was humming a song from the musical.

"So, you're going to be in the chorus? I thought you hated to sing," she said.

"I don't exactly hate to sing, I just haven't ever tried very hard," I said. "I'm trying something new. Aren't you the one who's always pestering me to try new things?"

"Sure," she said. "I'm really happy for you. I was worried about you feeling left out, anyway, so this way it's best for everyone." She sang out loud all the way to school, and I stopped feeling sorry for myself about last night.

The first class of the day I had with Sara was

phys ed. We were doing a unit on archery. How it fits into physical education is a mystery to me, unless you count how much your index and middle finger on your right hand hurt when you're through. It was raining the Seattle kind of rain that you either get used to or just ignore. It's more like a heavy mist all around you, like you're standing inside a rain cloud instead of underneath one. You don't get wet, exactly, just damp through to your bones. The moisture was making the bow slippery, and I was having a hard time hitting anywhere on the big, hay-stuffed bull's-eye out in the field.

"This is so boring, I think I'm going to die," Sara said, pounding the tip of an arrow into the gravel next to me. "Let's go run around the track a few times."

"I'd rather be bored than running," I said. Sara didn't admit to being bored very often, and when she did, you had to watch out, because she'd try just about anything. "Here, you try," I said, and handed her the bow. When the monitor gave the signal, I walked out past the target to retrieve the arrows. Before I even got back a group of kids had gathered around Sara and were giggling. She was pointing a strung bow and arrow at Billy Adams.

"Sara!" I hollered. She'd gone overboard, and besides that, she could get suspended for something like this, and thrown out of the play.

She turned to look at me and then I saw that the arrow was not pointed at Billy Adams, but right at her own chest.

"Say you love me, Billy," she said. "Say you love me right now or I'll die."

Billy stood there, pale to the tips of his ears instead of red this time. The other kids looked nervously back and forth from Sara and Billy to the teacher, who had his back to us, watching the soccer game on the far field.

"Say it, Billy," Sara said, pulling the bow tighter. "Say you love me." She squeezed two real tears out of one eye.

Billy shoved his hands deep down in his pockets and shifted his weight from one foot to the other. His large Adam's apple bobbed up and down along his pencil neck.

"Knock it off, Sara," he said, his voice an octave higher than normal.

"I'm not bluffing, Billy. You've always been my true love and I can't live any longer without your love in return." I was about to explode from holding in the giggles.

Billy looked at me in desperation, obviously considering that she might well do it. I just shrugged my shoulders, anxious to see what she'd do next, and trying not to lose it.

"Say it!" she shouted, convincingly hysterical.

"I love you!" Billy blurted out, sending a wave of uncomfortable laughter through the crowd. My eyes watered and I held my breath to keep from becoming completely unglued.

"Really?" Sara said, lowering her bow. "Now that that's settled, I'll sure rest easier at night." I shouldn't have tried to hold in my laughing, because I was completely out of control now. Sara grabbed the arrows out of my hand just as I sat down on the ground so I wouldn't pee my pants. I calmed down and felt the cold wetness soaking through my sweatpants to my skin. I'd sat in a puddle. I sat there, not moving, wondering what to do and watching Sara shoot.

"Let's go," she said. "Do you think Billy will ever forgive me?"

"No, and I don't think I will either," I said. "You made me laugh so hard, I had a little problem." She looked at me sitting on the ground and her eyes widened as she put two and two together. She knelt down next to me.

"Did you—"

"No!" I said. "But I sat in a puddle."

"Oh, man, sorry," she said, and put her hand over her mouth, where I suspected she was hiding a smile.

"Just help me out here. I don't know what to do," I said. "Everyone will think the same thing as you!"

"Okay, think, think, think . . . got it!" She pulled her oversize sweatshirt up over her head leaving her with nothing but her white underwire bra. "Here, slide up a little. We'll tie this around your waist and no one will be able to tell."

"But, Sara, you're naked!" I whispered.

"Not totally," she said as I tied the sleeves in a tight knot around my waist. "Just walk forward and look straight ahead like nothing weird's going on." I did what she said, and we didn't run into anyone on the way until we crossed the wide sidewalk before the locker rooms, almost to safety. Then Mr. Sanchez, the principal, came around the corner in his golf cart, which he uses because he's too heavy and out of shape to walk the length of campus, and nearly ran us over. We found ourselves in his office less than twenty minutes later after I'd changed.

"Well, you see, Mr. Sanchez, Amy peed in her pants, and I thought the sight of that would be far more offensive than the sight of me in my bra," said Sara. She leaned forward and lowered her voice. "And Amy is very sensitive, you know. She might have been traumatized. Permanently."

Mr. Sanchez stared at Sara and pressed his eyebrows together. I felt a burn starting at my toes, traveling through my body and up to my face like mercury rising. I dropped my head and willed the hot blood to drain from my face. I wanted to be as brave as Sara, but I could hardly even look at Mr. Sanchez, let alone talk about things like walking around in my bra like it was an overdue assignment or something.

A croaking sound came from Mr. Sanchez. He cleared his throat. "Perhaps you could have gone to the locker room and brought her out a *towel?*"

"That would have been a very good idea, but I just didn't think of it," Sara said.

Mr. Sanchez sat quietly for a long time. My face was still hot. When I looked up he stared at me level for a few seconds, then knit his fingers together and cracked his knuckles loud.

"I guess no harm has been done. But I don't want to see either of you in here the rest of the year. Understand?"

I nodded my head, got up fast, and made a beeline for the door. Sara shook Mr. Sanchez's hand and said thanks for his understanding and, yes, she would make sure nothing like this would ever happen again. She put her arm around my shoulders and we walked out into the hall together.

"Thanks for saving us," I said.

"I only saved myself. They can't give you detention for incontinence."

"Thanks anyway," I said.

A group of boys standing around the water fountain saw us coming and started laughing and catcalling. Word had obviously gotten around. I walked faster, ignoring them, but Sara went right on through them to the fountain. She cupped her hands under the water and threw it into the face of the closest boy.

"Anybody else?" she asked. Everyone backed up, but no one said anything, except the drenched boy who was swearing under his breath and wiping his glasses on his pants. She threw another handful of water at no one in particular and scattered the crowd.

Chapter 7

ONE AFTERNOON Ms. Newman brought a deep cardboard box into the back room.

"Here's your kitten, Amy," she said. "It's a him."

I'd almost forgotten. Inside the box was the black kitten with the white spot around his nose. I laughed when I saw him. He was a funny-looking thing, even more so now that he was bigger.

On the way home from school, I carried the box carefully because the kitten was asleep, curled up on the newspapers in the corner of the box. It made me nervous to bring something home I was going to be responsible for. I set the box down gently in the corner of the living room, made sure the kitten was still asleep, and left for the grocery store. I made a mental list on the way: kitty litter, cat food, tuna fish, and a little dish for his water. Maybe a brush, too.

The aisle with all the pet products overwhelmed me. I put a box of specially formulated-for-kittens food in the cart and stared at the rest of the products, wondering what else I needed.

"Amy!"

I nearly leaped out of my skin.

"Amy, how are you?" I turned and there was Ray, a friend from the second grade. He'd moved to another district, but I still saw him around once in a while.

"I'm fine," I said. "Sara's fine, too, the same as ever." Ray wasn't particularly interested in how I was doing—he'd been in love with Sara as long as I could remember. In the seventh grade, he nearly knocked himself out trying to get her attention, but Sara always thought his ears stuck out too far, he talked through his nose, and he was too short. She said she couldn't imagine kissing him unless it was the way Snow White kisses Dopey at the end of the movie, on top of the head and in a sisterly kind of way. Sara had brushed Ray off in the nicest way possible several times, but he still had hopes.

"Does she have a boyfriend?" he asked.

I shook my head. He smiled.

"So, you guys still catching frogs?" he asked. I'd forgotten he was privy to the whole "frog girls" episode.

"What do you think?" I asked. I didn't feel right lying to Ray, but it seemed funny to tell him the truth.

"Knowing you two, probably," he said.

I shrugged my shoulders. "Do you know anything about kittens? I just got one and don't know what I'm doing."

"Don't feed it milk," he said. "It'll get the runs. Will you say hello to Sara for me? Tell her I'd like to see her sometime soon."

"Sure, Ray," I said. "I will."

After he left, I decided on a few cans of cat food plus the box I already had in my cart. I bought a little collar, a dish, and a toy mouse.

When I got close to my house, there was somebody standing on the doorstep, trying to see inside through the little side window. I clutched my bag closer to me when I recognized Peter. Why did I have this reaction? I'd known him for a long time, but since that day at the tryouts, my stomach did flips every time I saw him. He rang the doorbell, waited a moment, and then started walking away.

"Peter!" I called, and ran to try and catch up. He turned and that smile of his lit up his face.

"Hey, I was looking for you," Peter said.

"Why?" I asked.

He looked uncomfortable. "No reason. I wanted to see you, that's all." He blushed a little. "I hope you don't mind I came to your house."

The fact that he actually blushed reassured me in a way, that I wasn't the only one who was unsure of my feelings.

"No, I'm glad you did," I said. My heart pounded and I could feel that my face was red, but it was a good uncomfortable feeling. "Come in and see my new kitten. Ms. Newman gave him to me."

"Can I carry the bag for you?" he asked.

"Chivalry and everything," I said, my stomach flipping again when his arm brushed mine as he took the bag. Before I opened the door, I closed my eyes and hoped I'd picked up the house. Lately, it got so I didn't even notice when it was a complete disaster.

We went in. The house wasn't too bad, except for the pile of laundry in the middle of the hall, which luckily contained Dad's jeans and shirts and not our underwear or something embarrassing.

"What did you name it?" Peter asked.

"I haven't decided yet," I said. "Maybe you can help me think of something."

The box was on its side and the kitten was gone.

"Oh, no! He was asleep when I left! He's so little! How did he knock over the box?" I began looking under and behind sofas and chairs.

"It's okay, Amy, I'm sure he's fine. We'll find him," Peter said.

We searched the room together, until we'd turned over every cushion and even looked through the laundry pile. I finally sat down, giving up, my head in my hands. Peter sat down next to me.

"Amy . . . ," he began, ". . . hang on. . . . Look at this!"

I looked up and he pointed up to the curtain rod. There was the kitten, sitting on top, looking calmly down on us. I jumped up.

"How on earth . . . ?" I grabbed a footstool so I could reach him and gently brought him down. "How on earth did a little thing like you get out of that big box and clear up there?"

"I've got a name for him," Peter said. "How about Houdini?"

"It seems appropriate," I said.

"Geez, will you look at the big nose on that thing!" Peter said, and laughed.

"Careful, you'll hurt his feelings," I said.

"I've got to get home," Peter said. "I'll see you at practice tomorrow?"

"Yeah, I'll see you tomorrow." I held Houdini in my hands and stroked his back with my thumb. He curled up and purred. "Thanks for helping me find him."

"No problem," he said, and leaned over and kissed my cheek so lightly I wasn't even sure afterward if it really happened. He was out the door before I could react. I was so light-headed, my head felt detached from my body. It was a long time since I felt truly happy in this room, in this house. Could pain and happiness exist in one space, in one room, in one body?

When Dad came home a little later, I was sitting on the couch, with the kitten stretched out across my legs.

"What have we got here?" he asked.

"I'm sorry, I should have asked first," I said. "Ms. Newman gave him to me. I saw him and wanted to bring him home. I don't know why. Is it okay?"

"I don't see why not," he said, and reached out and touched the kitten's stomach. A small smile crept on Dad's face. Did my dad ever feel happiness over his pain? I wondered if that's why he worked so hard and so long. How could listening to other people's problems all day help him?

"Amy, can we talk about something?" Dad began. He looked me in the eyes, which surprised me. It had been a long time since we'd looked at each other.

"Sure, Dad," I said.

"I know I'm gone a lot," he said. "Are you all right with that?"

I nodded my head.

"You haven't told me what you're up to lately. Are you keeping busy?"

"I have a heavy load at school, and I'm in the school musical. Just a chorus part," I said.

His eyes lit up. "Good, good. It's important to do healthy things with your time."

"Sara and I hang out, too, you know," I said, "but I'm alone a lot." I'm not sure why I added this last bit. I didn't want Dad to feel guilty or anything.

"What I do is important work," he said.

I nodded again.

"It helps me heal. And I think you would heal better, too, if you came back to church," he said.

"I don't want to," I said. "I don't like the way people look at me. And Mom . . . Mom is everywhere in that building because it was such a huge part of her life. I can't stand it."

Dad looked like he wanted to say something else, but he wasn't one to push. We sat for a moment, neither quite willing to let go of the first real conversation we'd had in a long time.

"Have you abandoned everything?" he asked. His voice was soft and restrained. "I think I can understand a little of your wanting to avoid the building and the people, although I don't think it's right, especially in the long run. And especially knowing how much all the congregation cares about you. But what I'm most worried about is your faith in God, your beliefs—you haven't abandoned them, have you?"

I hesitated and then told the truth. "I don't know." Dad's face looked pained and he looked down. "I don't think so."

I thought about how happy I was just a little while ago with Peter. Any happiness we had could only be momentary, because there was always the horrible, horrible loss that we could never forget.

Dad sat down in the chair across from me and we sat in silence, watching the kitten breathe, forgetting about dinner, until the dark blue night shadows closed in and chilled us. I brought the kitten up to bed with me because I was afraid if I left him alone again I wouldn't be able to find him.

"Good night, Dad," I said from the top of the stairs to the impenetrable darkness downstairs.

"Night, Amy," he said, and turned off the light.

Chapter 8

"I'D LOVE TO GO to the dance," Sara told my dad the next Saturday, "but only if Amy goes."

Dad smiled at me, kind of smug, knowing he'd won. We were eating dinner at my house, "dinner" being frozen bagel hot dogs and Tang. Lately he'd been trying to convince me to go to church functions, dances, and activities. It made me feel weird that he was coming out of his fog enough to worry about me. I was getting used to us living in our own cocoons. It seemed easier that way.

"I hate those things," I told Sara. "You know I hate those things."

"You do not. I've seen you have fun. We used to go all the time, and I really miss it. Just come to keep me company? I'd feel funny without you," she said. "You don't have anything else to do Friday night, do you?"

Sara and I went out every Friday night, usually to a movie. It was a given that we'd be together. We didn't even have to make plans; she'd show up at my house after dinner and we'd do whatever.

"No, but I still don't want to go."

"Tell you what," said Dad. "Just go for an hour with Sara, and then you two can do something you want to do. I'll let you take the car."

You have to hand it to Dad. How was I supposed to say no to that?

So we ended up at the dance, me wearing all brown, no makeup, and straightened hair, so I'd blend into the wall. Sara was in lime green and out on the dance floor, as usual. People say I'm pretty, and sometimes when I'm hanging around in the mall or walking down the street, I can turn some heads. But I can also look cold as anything, if I want to, and I was putting on my best frozen face.

On the other hand, if you were to look at Sara, not knowing her at all, you wouldn't necessarily say she was pretty. But she has a certain way of getting people to like her right off, even if she's not in one of her friendly moods. My dad claims it's "charisma." Whatever it is, it works, and she's usually the most popular person in the room. Me, I tend to hang back, but since Sara is my best friend, I'm in on everything like a fly on the wall almost. It suits me fine.

"Hey, Amy!" A voice startled me. I swung around and came face-to-face with Peter. "It couldn't be that bad, could it?"

"What are you talking about?" I asked, pushing my hair behind my ears and having the peculiar feeling I should have worn something more flattering.

"That scowl on your face. You want to talk about it?"

"No," I said, and then continued like an idiot, "my dad wanted me to come. I didn't want to be here. I came with Sara," I said, as if that explained everything.

We stood there without talking, both of us watching Sara. The song ended and she ran over to me and looped her arm through mine. "My hour's up. It's so hot in here, I'm dying. Let's go get a Coke. Ready?" she asked me.

Peter stood there smiling, looking like he wanted an invitation, but I didn't know what to say, so Sara said it for me.

"You coming, Peter?"

He looked at me and then back at Sara.

"I would love to, but I drove a group here, so I have to stick around."

Sara shrugged her shoulders and dragged me toward the door.

I tried to think of something clever to say. "Bye, Peter," I said. Brilliant.

"See you around, Amy. Maybe next time we can dance?"

I nodded my head as Sara pulled open the door.

The blast of cold air made my teeth sting because I was still smiling.

Maybe there was an overdose of caffeine in the Big Gulp I got from the 7-Eleven, but that night I couldn't sleep. Usually I sleep just fine at Sara's house, way better than I do at home. I had an uneasy feeling like some things were changing, although I couldn't quite put my finger on what. Maybe it was Dad starting to worry about what I did with my time. Maybe it was Sara and this musical. Maybe it was Peter. I had just gotten used to living with my pain; I had my ways of dealing with it. It was like I was lying on a bed of nails and I could tolerate it if I just kept perfectly still. Any move I made, however small, would open up new wounds.

I counted seconds like I do when I don't want to think, one, one thousand, two, one thousand, and sank into the beginning of sleep, somewhere after one hundred twenty-one one-thousand. But before I hit the point of no return, still in that floaty stage, something welled up in my chest and the memory of myself as a six-year-old following my mother closely through a store chased away sleep. We were shopping for my birthday present, but I couldn't make up my mind. All the dolls and stuffed animals and games overwhelmed me and made me feel panicky.

"Pick something for me, Mom, please," I remember saying.

"Don't be silly," she told me. "It's your birthday. You pick something you like." We walked up and down the aisles again, Mom looking at me hopefully when I picked up a pink box containing a blond long-haired Barbie. She had three changes of clothes and a little curling iron and high-heeled shoes.

"There's something nice," Mom said. "Is that what you would like?"

I put it back and started to cry. "I don't know." I expected Mom to hug me and tell me it was all right, and that she would choose something for me after all. But instead she bent down and put her hands firmly on my shoulders and looked straight into my eyes.

"Amy, no one else can tell you what you want," she told me.

I opened my eyes and stared at Sara's basement ceiling, at the little points of glitter stuck on the water-stained asbestos, feeling that same sense of panicky uncertainty. I tried to empty my mind and concentrated on Sara's sleeping, rhythmic breathing. I timed my own breathing to hers and eventually slept.

Chapter 9

A SCREAMING SMOKE DETECTOR jerked us awake and sent us running for our robes. We struggled to strap on our shoes by the door—the ones we had worn to the dance.

We didn't smell any smoke, or see any flames, and by then the only shrieking came from Dorothy.

"Get out! Get out!" she screamed, shoving us out the door.

Now Sara and I stood in the middle of the cul-de-sac, shivering in our bathrobes and high heels. I wondered why I bothered to put the shoes on. My toes were turning blue. A few brown leaves scraped by our feet.

"She always exaggerates," said Sara. "She's hysterical. There's no fire."

"I don't think even your mother could exaggerate a smoke alarm," I said.

"She probably set it off herself with her cigarette. Anything for drama," Sara said, and crunched a leaf under her foot. "I'll bet it's about four-thirty."

Two hours of sleep. I guess I was still riding the adrenaline wave because I wasn't tired.

"Four-thirty in the morning in the middle of October. Couldn't she have picked, say, July, in the afternoon? I wonder what she's doing in there?"

We looked toward Sara's house where we had been sleeping two minutes earlier.

"Do you think they'll send paramedics?" asked Sara. "Mom's hoping they'll send paramedics. She says they're always better-looking than the firemen."

"Why would anyone send paramedics? There's not even a fire," I said, self-conscious in my cruddy robe and smashed-down hair.

"Oh, you wait. She'll have the whole emergency division of Seattle out here," she said.

A dark figure on a bike turned the corner of the cul-de-sac. The brakes squeaked, and the Sunday paper hit the neighbor's door with a loud *thunk*.

"It's Peter," I whispered, and stood behind Sara. "I'm going to die. I'm going to *die!* Hide me!"

66

"Calm down, Amy. It's dark. He might not even see you."

I tried to hunker down behind Sara, even though I'm half a head taller. The bike pulled up next to us.

"Hey," said Peter.

"Hi!" said Sara. "Amy's trying to hide because her hair looks stupid."

"Thanks a lot," I said, and punched her on the arm. Peter was looking at me, and he had that crooked grin on his face. He pushed his own hair back from the one eye it always covered.

"What are you doing out here?" he asked.

"There was a fire . . ." I began.

Peter sniffed the air and looked around the silent neighborhood.

"Well, I mean the smoke alarm went off."

"I see," he said, grinning so big his face nearly cracked in two.

The front door of the house flew open and Sara's mom came out and stood under the streetlight up close to the house. She was wearing a black flowing robe, matching slippers, and jewelry. It looked like her face and hair were done up, too.

"Just kill me now," said Sara as the fire trucks, sirens blaring, rounded the corner.

The first fire truck parked in front of the house and a pudgy short guy with an overgrown mustache hopped out of the truck. I guessed if he took his hat off he wouldn't have much hair.

"What's the problem here?" he asked Sara and me as doors slammed and more firefighters jumped out of trucks.

"The only problem is her," said Sara, and pointed toward her mother.

The firefighter nodded as if this were an acceptable answer and jogged over to Dorothy.

"Not her type," Sara said. She sat down on the curb and pretended to sleep with her arms crossed over her knees and head down.

"Well, I guess I better finish delivering my papers," said Peter. He pulled his bike up real close to me and reached his hand out like he wanted to touch my scrunched-up hair, but then his bike tipped and he had to steady the handlebars. He put his foot on the pedal and rolled away a little.

"I meant what I said about dancing with you sometime," he said, and then rode away.

I worried about the butterflies in my stomach. He was friends with everyone I was trying to avoid. He went to church. He knew my dad and my mom and all their friends. He believed stuff I used to believe and now don't think about.

The fire trucks drove away and the morning light filtered through the tall pine trees that bordered the neighborhood. I wanted to crawl back in bed and avoid even the light. Sara and Dorothy decided to go out for breakfast. I gathered my things and went home and tried to go back to sleep, but that half dream of my six-year-old self came back.

Why hadn't I just chosen that Barbie in the pink box?

And then I remembered we left the store without anything.

Chapter 10

WHAT SARA TOLD ME about being gone a lot because of the musical turned out to be true. I only had two practices a week, since I was in the chorus, but Sara had something practically every day after school. And when she wasn't actually at a practice, she talked about it, which meant Anita usually came up in the conversation. I couldn't help but wish this musical would get over quickly so things could get back to normal. Except Mondays and Wednesdays. I found myself looking forward to seeing Peter.

Monday at practice I made sure my hair looked good and I wore something halfway decent, to make up for the fire alarm incident. I wanted Peter to notice me. I came into practice a little late because I spent too long in the bathroom trying to rub a pen mark from art class off my chin, so I had to sit on the edge of the group, about four people away from Peter. He looked over and smiled at me. I hoped my chin wasn't red from all the rubbing.

"Today, we're going to do something a little different," Mr. Alberts said. "I've noticed some of you are carrying the rest. I want everyone to contribute equally. A few strong voices and a lot of weak ones don't make a good chorus. So, I'll ask each of you today to sing solo. Get used to contributing to your part, as if you were the only one performing."

I felt a little sick. I didn't have the greatest voice in the world, and of course Peter had heard me sing next to him, but today it seemed different. I couldn't remember feeling this self-conscious in a long time. As Mr. Alberts went down each row, having each person sing a section of the song, I avoided eye contact with Peter. I took deep breaths instead, hoping to calm down before my turn. Mr. Alberts started at the far end of my row. That meant Peter would have to go before me. Good. I looked down at my hands when it was his turn.

I heard a loud, clear note, and then it sounded like Peter choked or something. I looked over at him, along with everyone else. He put his hand to his mouth and cleared his throat.

"Sorry. Let's try again," he said, barely audible. He cleared his throat again and started. His singing was nice, this time, but still a little shaky. I felt bad for him, but relieved because now I didn't feel like my own singing had to be so perfect.

When my turn came, I started right in, not looking at anyone. My voice sounded far away, like I was lip-synching to someone else's song. Then it was over and I looked back down at my hands. I could feel Peter's eyes on me and my face felt warm. Finally, I looked over and he gave me a thumbs-up.

"That was much better," Mr. Alberts said. "Now, let's sing together."

The rest of practice went by fast, and I kept Peter in the corner of my eye. I caught him looking at me a few times.

"Boy, I really goofed up," Peter said afterward. "I told you I wasn't a great singer."

"You did just fine," I said. "I'm not a singer either. Why are we in this thing, anyway?"

He shrugged his shoulders. "Got me."

We stood there, neither one of us knowing what to say next. We weren't used to hanging out together unless you count sitting in the same congregation at church or him chasing me around in third grade.

"You want to grab some burgers?" he asked me.

"Um, yeah, sure," I stammered. "I don't have any money on me, though. Maybe we could run by my house. . . ."

"My treat," he said. "Paper-route money. It's not a great-paying job, but it's worth it. Like when I see people standing around in their jammies and dressy shoes."

"I'm so embarrassed," I said.

"You didn't need to hide from me," he said. "I thought you looked beautiful."

My stomach did a three-sixty. "Only because it was dark," I said. I wondered if I got all the pen off my chin. Could he see I was blushing? "But thanks."

Peter seemed embarrassed, too, but he didn't take his eyes off me. "I've always thought so."

"Thanks," I said again. Why wouldn't my brain work? Say something smart, I thought.

"Here comes Sara," Peter said. "Should we invite her along?"

I turned around and saw Sara, along with Anita.

"It looks like we'll have to invite Anita, too," I said.

"That'd be fine," Peter said.

It wasn't really, but at least I would have better things to worry about than flypaper girl.

Peter and I slid into one bench at the hamburger place and Sara and Anita sat opposite us. Sara and

Peter ordered shakes, fries, and burgers, and I ordered a burger and a shake because whenever Sara and I came here, we shared an order of fries. It was tradition. Anita only wanted a Diet Coke.

"You should eat something," Sara said.

"Okay, Mom," Anita said. "I'll eat one of your fries. That's all the fat grams I can handle."

"You worry too much," Sara said. "You look great!"

I wondered if I should have ordered less, since Peter was paying, but he leaned over and whispered into my ear, "Why don't girls like Anita eat? I like girls with a healthy appetite." What a relief. Maybe I should have ordered a double burger.

"Don't let her fool you. I'll bet she's going to eat a gallon of ice cream when she gets home," I whispered back. Where was this meanness coming from? Did I really wish an eating disorder on someone?

"Hey, Eric!" Anita shouted across two booths. "Eric! Over here!"

A tall boy wearing a football jersey from another school came over.

"Hey, 'Nita," he said.

"This is my cousin Eric," Anita said. "Eric, this is Amy, Peter, and my best friend, Sara." Best friend?

"How's it going?" Eric said to me and Peter. To Sara he said, "I've heard all about you."

Our food came, and I busied myself getting straws and ketchup. When I got back to the table and sat down, Peter slung his arm over my shoulders, even though it made it awkward for him to eat. I tried not to tense my shoulders. I wanted Peter to think I was entirely comfortable this way, although I was hyperconscious of him touching me. I squirted a pool of ketchup on my plate for the fries.

While Eric, Sara, and Anita talked, I focused on Peter being so close to me, touching me, and tried to ignore the "best friend" comment by Anita. She could think whatever she wanted. When Eric finally went away, I expected Sara to dump half her fries on my plate, like always. But she didn't. Instead she twirled her plate around, so the fries were between her and Anita. Embarrassed by the ketchup on my plate, I cut my burger in pieces with my knife and dipped those in the ketchup instead. I tried to act happy, and I was, as far as Peter was concerned, but inside I caught myself wishing the three fries Anita ate from Sara's dish would go straight to her hips.

Chapter 11

"MY MOM'S GIVEN UP on the fire department," Sara told me a few days later. "Now she's dating a ferry captain."

"Oh, sorry," I said. Usually Sara hated anyone her mom dated.

"No, it's okay. Mom says we get to ride the ferries for free. We're going to Salt Spring Island Saturday and you can come if you want."

"Yeah, I'd love to," I said. Salt Spring Island was one of my favorite places on the planet. Besides, it would be good to be together without anyone else, because I was still steamed from the other night at the hamburger place.

It's not that I minded Sara having other friends. I mean, she was one of the most popular kids in the school. It's just she didn't need any other real close friends because we had each other. There wasn't room for anyone else to have the kind of friendship I shared with her. You can't have a very-best-friend-no-secrets kind of closeness with more than one person. And Sara and I would always be that kind of friends. Why didn't Anita get it? And why did I worry so much? It's like our feet were planted in cement together. It would take an earthquake to break us apart.

That afternoon, Peter didn't show up for practice so the whole thing felt like torture. There didn't seem to be any reason to be there without him.

"Amy, you want to catch a ride home with Anita and me?" Sara asked. Anita stood behind Sara, snapping her gum. She was still dressed in her cheerleading uniform. Mrs. VanSickle let her come late to practices so they wouldn't interfere with the JV football games that took place in the afternoon.

"No thanks, I'm going to walk," I said.

"Are you sure?" Sara asked. "Anita doesn't mind at all."

"Are you speaking for Anita now?" I asked

"What's that supposed to mean?" Anita said. Sara gave me a funny look.

"Nothing. Really. I'm going to walk over to my dad's office, so I'll see you guys later." I left and started walking, kicking rocks along the way. I didn't really want to see Dad, but I didn't have anywhere else to go, and besides, Peter's house was on the way.

I don't know what I expected to happen when I walked by Peter's house. It didn't look like anyone was home, and I didn't get too close anyway because I wouldn't know what to say if he saw me and came out or something. I could see my dad's office a block away. Parked out front was Dorothy's red Impala. I walked a little closer, remembering the envelope I'd found in her purse, and what Sara had said about her mother and my dad. I still didn't believe it, and after all, she was dating the ferry captain. I got close enough to see the front door a little ajar, and Dorothy standing with her back pressed against it, talking to someone inside. She walked out, followed by Dad. My throat got tight and I half expected them to hug each other. But Dad stuck out his hand and they shook hands, standing a respectable distance apart. She walked to her car and Dad waved and went back in.

It didn't appear anything fishy was going on, outside the fact I couldn't imagine what Dorothy would be doing here.

Dorothy's car pulled a U-turn and drove straight toward me. I had to keep walking because there was nothing else I could do. She pulled up next to me, leaned over, and swung the passenger door open.

"Amy! Hop in!" she said.

"No thanks," I said.

"Were you going to see your dad?" she asked.

"Well," I looked over at his office. I wondered if she knew I saw her. I didn't think so. "No, not really."

"Come on, I'll give you a ride. I'm picking up a pizza on the way home. You can come back to our house and eat with us. Mushrooms are your favorite, right?"

My stomach grumbled. "Only if you get an extra-large," I said.

"What other choice is there?" she asked. I decided not to ask her what she was doing here because I didn't want to spoil things and wasn't sure I wanted to know, anyway. And she wasn't offering any explanations.

Just getting a pizza turned into about seven other chores. We stopped and bought toothpaste, picked up some stuff at the dry cleaners, and dropped off mail at the post office. We didn't talk much. I was busy feeling bad about being left out. I knew I was reacting like a baby—it was me, after all, who refused the ride with Sara and Anita. But I couldn't shake the fact they didn't want me with them. By the time we finally pulled into Sara's driveway, it was dark and I was starving.

Sara met us at the door, her eyes red and puffy.

"Amy, I've been so worried!" she said, and threw her arms around me. Dorothy put the pizza down on the front stairs.

"What's the matter, Sara?" she asked.

"Amy said she was walking over to her dad's office, and I tried to call her there, and her dad said she never came, so I called her house and . . ." Sara took a deep breath, pulled back, and put her hands on my shoulders. "And you weren't there either. You seemed mad when you left. I was worried."

I didn't know quite what to say. Sara's reaction was over the top.

"Well, we're all here in one piece, and we've got a pizza to eat," Dorothy said, and went in.

Sara was still staring at me.

"I . . . I wasn't mad, exactly," I started, and then launched into it. This was Sara, not some stranger who wouldn't understand. "I'm just annoyed that Anita's constantly around, and I never get to see you anymore without her being there."

I expected Sara to crack a joke or do something funny. She's good at breaking up tension that way. But instead she started crying again.

"It's okay, it's not the end of the world," I said. Sara was freaking me out. "As soon as the musical is over, everything will be back to normal, and, hey, Anita's not so bad, except maybe the pom-poms. Sara, really, I'm okay. What is the matter with you?"

She hugged me close again and said, "I just don't want to cause you any pain."

"The only thing that hurts right now is my stomach. I'm starving," I said. "Let's go eat."

Sara nodded her head and then blew her nose loudly into the hem of her shirt.

"That's disgusting," I said. "How am I supposed to eat now?"

"More for me," Sara said, and then smiled.

Chapter 12

SATURDAY WE DROVE NORTH from Seattle, through Bellingham, and over the Canadian border where you catch the ferries to the gulf islands. It's a pretty drive, about two hours from Seattle, but it doesn't seem very long, especially when you're with Dorothy and Sara and blasting Dorothy's R&B tapes.

Sara and I got out of the car and headed for the terminal. Dorothy stood outside the car in the wind and tried to light a cigarette. I took in a deep breath until I could taste the salt water in the wind.

"I've got to use the bathroom," Sara said. "Meet me in the gift shop."

In the terminal they had a shop with sculptures of seagulls on driftwood and snow globes with little moose and Canadian Mounties in them. There was a rack with key chains that looked like Washington State license plates with names on them. I found Amy and Sara, except Sara had an *h* on the end, and then looked for Peter's name. When I found it I picked it up and turned it around in my hand.

"What have you got there?" Sara surprised me.

"Nothing. Just looking at this stuff," I said, and hung the key chain back on its post.

"If you're going to get tacky souvenirs," Sara said, "then make sure it's truly tacky. You don't want anyone to think you have plain bad taste." She looked around the shop.

"Take this spoon with the picture of the ferry on the handle." She held it up for me to see. "High-class tack. Kitsch, even. Or this moose mug. This is the kind of thing only a connoisseur of the horrible could appreciate."

"All right, I get your point. But I think the moose is kind of cute," I said.

"Let's go before I lose you completely," she said, and pushed open the door.

"So you really have a thing for Peter?" Sara asked. We were standing outside the ferry terminal, letting the wind whip our hair. I watched a gull pick apart and swallow a hot dog bun that was smashed into the pavement.

"I want to either throw up or jump on him every time I see him."

"Hmmm . . ." she said, pulling a strand of hair from her mouth. "I wish I felt that way about Peter."

I punched her on the arm. "Don't tell that to Ray," I said. "He's been knocking himself out trying to get your attention."

"Hmmm . . ." she said again, and made a face.

The ferry arrived, this one named *The Queen Naimo*, with its unmistakable honk, like a foghorn. Dorothy sat in the car while we waited as walk-ons. We watched the rows of cars drive off the lower deck into the customs terminal where they ask you if you're bringing in any fruit or alcohol. Then a man in an orange vest smoking a cigarette waved us through and we boarded the ferry.

"Thank you very much," Sara said to the man, "and I must say you look spectacular in Day-Glo." The man opened his mouth to say something, but the cigarette dropped into the pocket of his vest. He started dancing a jig and whapping himself on the chest to put it out.

I grabbed Sara's arm and moved her along.

"Why do you do things like that?" I asked when we were safely inside.

"So you'll think I'm funny. I saw you laughing."

I rolled my eyes.

We headed straight for the restaurant. The ferries are big and clean, and pretty smooth sailing. The only time you really notice the rocking is when you have your tray full of food, and you have to be careful not to tip it.

The line at the restaurant was long. It was past dinnertime and everyone had been stuck waiting for the late ferry. Sara and I always order the same thing—fries, a big platter each, and a guava and raspberry juice drink with the label all in French. The fries are smothered in gravy, which is way better than ketchup.

I pulled out my American dollars. The cashier rings it up in Canadian dollars first, then presses a button on the cash register and it subtracts about 30 percent. Sara always changes her money before we come, but I like to pay with American dollars. That way you feel like you're getting a deal.

"I'd like to own a house out here," Sara said. She pointed out the window to a small island with about three homes, very far apart, set on steep cliffs. I wondered how the owners got to them. Maybe there were hidden roads on the other side. We ate in silence for a while, watching the islands turn shades of gold and deep auburn in the setting sun.

I scraped up the rest of the gravy on my plate with the last of my fries, and then picked at Sara's while she stared out the window.

"I love to watch the sun go down here," Sara said. "It's so different from the city, like there's a different kind of end to the day."

I kept quiet.

"It would be nice to be alone for a while, all alone," she said. I was a little offended at this. Being together all the time like we were was just the same as being alone to me, actually much better.

"Yeah, but you'd miss civilization," I said, picking up our trays and dumping the trash.

We went out to the front deck. The air was warm here, not what you would expect from islands not too far from the cold and dampness of Puget Sound.

We watched the last of the sunset, first pink and then orange. The wind picked up our hair from the back and blew it straight up.

"Amy, do you remember earlier what I asked about how you feel about Peter? How I wished I felt that way about somebody?"

"Yeah," I said, confused. "Did you change your mind about Ray?"

"No," she said, quiet. She pressed her lips together and then said, "I think I do like someone like that. It's kind of this feeling in the pit of my stomach."

"Like you're going to throw up, right?"

"Yeah, like that."

"Who is it?" I asked.

"I'll let you know if I actually throw up."

"Come on, out with it," I said.

"I have to be absolutely sure, first," she said.

She smoothed her hair back off her forehead with both hands, pulling her skin tight and her eyebrows up.

"Whaddya say we go buy some chocolate?" She let her hair go and it blew into her mouth and eyes as she nearly ran to the door.

"Just so long as I'm the first to know!" I shouted as I followed behind her.

That night at the bed-and-breakfast, Dorothy, Sara, and I stayed up late and watched videos in our room and ordered in Chinese.

"Isn't the homecoming dance soon?" Dorothy asked.

"Next week," said Sara. "Two days after the musical. It's weird the school planned two big events that close together."

"Next week? You're kidding!" I said as if I didn't know. I had been hoping, actually kind of assuming, that Peter would ask me to go with him.

Sara flopped back on the bed. "I can't believe Billy didn't ask me to go to homecoming with him. You know he loves me." She laughed. "Ray asked me to go to his homecoming, which is the same night. I had to say no. Haven't I been clear enough with that boy?"

"Poor Ray," I said. "He'll try again next year."

"No, he won't. We got into a fight. Nooooo, he won't be asking me out again, probably ever."

"What'd you fight about?" I asked.

"Who knows. Nothing. Everything." She changed the subject. "I'm guessing Peter hasn't asked you, then."

"No." I shrugged my shoulders so they would think I didn't care.

"Does he have another girlfriend?" Dorothy asked.

"No!" I said. "At least I don't think so." Did he? I hadn't seen him much outside of school, and he'd been absent a few days lately. Maybe he was just being nice to me. Maybe he didn't care about me the way I thought. Maybe I was seeing things that weren't there.

"There's only one way to resolve this," Dorothy said. She got her wallet out of her purse and handed me her phone card. Then she put the telephone in my lap. "Ask him."

"I don't think so," I said and put the phone on the floor. I'd rather have bamboo shoved under my fingernails.

"Come on, Amy, you know he likes you," said Sara. "It's written all over his face every time he sees you."

"Then why hasn't he asked me?" I said. "And he hasn't been to practice lately. Maybe he's avoiding me altogether."

"Who knows?" said Dorothy. "Who knows how the male brain works. I wasn't exactly planning to have a slumber party with you two tonight, so don't ask me. Call him, Amy. It's the sanest thing you could do."

Dorothy was so different from my own mother but at the moment she seemed to make perfect sense.

"Do it, Amy." Sara put the phone back in my lap. Of course I had Peter's number memorized, even though I'd never called him, so I dialed quickly before I chickened out.

I panicked as the phone rang, wondering what I'd do if I woke up his mom or dad.

"Hello?" I nearly choked, but felt relieved at the same time. It was Peter.

"Hello. Peter. It's Amy," I said.

"Hey, Amy. What's going on?" he asked.

"I know it's weird that I'm calling you so late, but I'm sitting here in Salt Spring Island with Dorothy and Sara and . . ."

"You're where?" Peter sounded completely confused.

I took a deep breath to calm myself. "Peter, I just wanted to know if you want to go to the home-coming dance with me." There, I'd said it.

There was a long pause and I heard sheets rustle. I must have woken him up. My hands got clammy and my head felt hot. He must be trying to come up with some excuse.

"I'd love to. When is it?" he finally said.

"Next Saturday," I said. My voice squeaked because I was so excited and relieved.

"Amy, I was going to ask you, but I've had this flu and just kind of lost track of things," he said. I imagined his big crooked grin and felt better. He'd been sick. And he wanted to go to the dance with me.

"Will you do me a favor?" I asked. "Will you check on Houdini tomorrow morning? I don't trust my dad to take care of him. Make sure he has fresh water, something to eat, and that his litter box doesn't have too many you-know-whats in it. He won't use it unless it's clean. That is, if you're feeling better."

"Only for you, Amy. Only for you would I check a cat's litter box," he said, and I could feel his grin through the phone.

Chapter 13

THE WEEK WENT QUICKLY with a flurry of rehearsals and getting ready for the dance. I found a dress at the mall one afternoon after rehearsal and it seemed perfect. I used a little money I had put away in my bank account. My feelings for Peter, though, were anything but perfect. Up until now, any real relationship with him seemed dreamlike, far away, and more like fantasy than real. Something still at arm's length. But seeing him every day at rehearsal, and knowing we were going to the dance together, and finally, buying a dress I thought he would like me in, made me think I might be complicating my already confusing existence. With the musical almost over, Anita wouldn't be so much of an issue, and Sara and I could go back to spending our time together. Did I need anything else?

Mostly, I didn't try and analyze stuff, I just tried to keep the butterflies in my stomach down and my thinking straight.

The night of the musical, most of the kids drove over with their parents. I'd forgotten to give Dad the date until that morning, and he'd arranged some sort of meeting he said he couldn't get out of, but he'd try to make it before it got too late. He was annoyed with me that I hadn't bothered to mention the date, but I'd pointed out that he hadn't asked either.

I walked over to the school by myself, feeling lonely, and it didn't get much better. I didn't get to be next to Peter in the chorus, and the way we were arranged, I couldn't see him either. Sara was brilliant, and even I had to admit Anita had a natural talent for performing. Must be all those hours behind her pom-poms. As the play went on, I felt happier and happier that it was almost at an end.

After the last number, the crowd went crazy and before I knew it, Sara and Anita and a few others were taking curtain calls. It was all over.

Peter ran over to me and gave me a hug. "It was great, don't you think?"

"I'm glad it's over, though!" I said. The hug felt good. What had I been worried about? At that moment it seemed Peter in my life afforded some clarity instead of confusion.

Then we were surrounded by Sandra and some of the other kids from church.

"Let's go celebrate!" Peter said.

"How about McGregor's Fountain?" Sandra said.

"Good. I'll drive. Meet me out front," Peter said. Then he turned to me. "Why don't you invite Sara and Anita, if you want. I'm going to pull my car around up front. Meet you outside."

"Wait . . . Peter." I had to chase him a few yards because he was moving quickly. I didn't want to go out with his group of friends. I wanted it to be just me and him or me and him and Sara. But how would I separate Sara and Anita? Or Peter from the others? I spotted Dad in the crowd. By the time I caught Peter's sleeve, I had my excuse.

"I can't come, Peter," I said. What had he been thinking, anyway, just assuming I would want to go? "I've got plans with my dad."

Peter looked disappointed, but his face brightened when my dad walked over.

"Great job, you guys," Dad said. "I only caught the last half, but it looks like I saw the best part."

"Thanks," Peter said. "The chorus didn't do so much, but it was fun to be part of the whole thing."

"We better be going, Dad," I said. I didn't want him to give away my lie.

"What's the rush?" Dad asked. "Would you like to join us for some sodas, Peter?"

Good. That sounded good.

"I'd love to, but I've already promised to drive a bunch to McGregor's. Why don't you and Amy join us, if it wouldn't mess up your plans," he said.

Dad looked at me. No, no, no, no, I willed him to say. There was something worse than being with the kids from church tonight. Being with my dad *and* the kids from church tonight.

"Why not?" Dad said. "Maybe we'll ride over in my car. . . ." I had to do something.

"Dad," I interrupted. "I was looking forward to spending time with you tonight, alone. I . . . I need to talk to you about something."

"I didn't mean to interfere," Peter said.

"Oh, no, you weren't interfering," I said to Peter. "I just had . . . other plans. I'm sorry."

"No need to be sorry," Peter said. "I'll catch you later?"

"Yeah, later," I said.

Peter leaned close and whispered in my ear, "I'm looking forward to the dance." And then he disappeared into the crowd and I was left alone with Dad.

"All right, then, Amy," he said. "Where would you like to go?"

"Anywhere but McGregor's," I said.

We decided on a small diner by our house. The ride over was quiet, both of us uncomfortable, I thought, with the silence.

After we'd ordered root beer floats, Dad said, "Well, what did you want to talk to me about?" His eyebrows were pinched together and he looked a little nervous.

I'd forgotten I said that. I did some quick thinking.

"How would you feel . . . ," I began, ". . . if I said I asked Peter to go to the homecoming dance with me?"

Dad sat back against the vinyl bench. His face relaxed and he took a long sip of his drink. "Is that all?" He laughed a little. "I'd say that's wonderful!"

"Glad you approve," I said. What on earth did he think I was going to say?

Chapter 14

ON SATURDAY MORNING I wondered if I'd made a huge mistake. I stared into my bowl of Cheerios and pushed each one down with the spoon, trying to make them stay at the bottom.

"So, you're going to the big dance tonight," Dad said. The Cheerios kept floating back to the top.

"Peter's a real nice kid," Dad started. "In fact, he's the most dependable young man in our entire congregation. You know, last year when we had that freak snowstorm, he shoveled Mrs. Foster's walk off every single morning. Nobody even had to ask him."

I thought I was going to be sick. His mother probably brought casseroles to people with a death in the family. I was launching myself right back into the scene I'd tried so hard to run away from. I was glad Peter was picking me up at my house. I couldn't stand to talk to his mom and dad and have them ask how I'm doing with this look in their eyes as if I was a lost puppy who needed their help.

"Amy?" Sara opened the door and stepped in just like she always does. Dad slipped around the corner so she wouldn't see him half-dressed.

"Hey, Sara, I'm glad you're here. I don't think I should go tonight. I don't think I really want this," I said. I didn't have to try to explain anything else. It's not like I could have if I wanted to. But Sara understood.

"You've got to. It's too late now to do anything about it," she said. "Besides, you bought that great dress."

I was feeling better already. The dress was a pale yellow and hung so I didn't look so skinny. Sara could put things in perspective like no one else. She opened the freezer and rummaged through all the mysterious things wrapped in foil and found some lemonade concentrate. She emptied out an almost-gone pitcher of orange juice from the fridge and washed it.

"You have to stop being afraid of things," she said as she dumped the concentrate into the clean pitcher. "Look at this as a first step to getting back to yourself."

"Thank you, Dr. Sara," I said. I wished she'd shut up now.

"No, really, I mean it. Peter makes you happy. Just go with it. I would love to see you happy again." She held the pitcher under the faucet and threw in some ice cubes.

"I am happy," I lied. And Sara knew it. "I mean, I'm fine the way things are. I'm not sure I want to change anything right now."

Sara opened her mouth to say something, but instead she just stirred the lemonade. The ice cubes clinked against the side of the pitcher.

"Amy, I'm just not sure that our friendship is enough for you. You've got to have something else, too," she finally said.

I ignored this. Our friendship was enough for me.

Sara put the lemonade in the refrigerator.

"Aren't you going to have some?" I asked.

"No. Maybe later," she said. "Let's go shopping for some shoes. You don't have anything decent. Can you get your dad's car?"

"Yeah, he's real excited about this whole dance thing. Wait here," I said, grateful for the diversion.

Dad was in the bathroom shaving. He did it the old-fashioned way, wetting a brush and foaming up some shaving soap he kept in an old mug. He spread it on his cheeks and neck and across the top of his mouth. He took out a big razor, pulled the skin on his neck taut, and started shaving under his jaw.

"Dad, can I take the car? I'm going shoe shopping."

He stopped shaving and said, "Hang on just a second." He disappeared into his bedroom and came out with a crumpled pair of pants. He dug through the pocket on one side and came up with the keys and two twenty-dollar bills. "Here you go. Have fun." The shaving soap formed a crust around his mouth and it cracked when he smiled. Really, he seemed almost happy this morning.

A twang of guilt raced through me, although I'm not exactly sure why. Maybe because he wasn't happy more often. Maybe it was because I could make things easier for him some way. Like cooking dinners like my mother used to. Like ironing his shirts the special way she did. But that would remind both of us of what we were missing.

I took the money—not enough for the mall, but I could pick up something at the discount store.

In the car, Sara asked, "So are you going to kiss Peter?"

"Wouldn't you?" I asked, smiling. I was over my morning funk and was actually feeling excited. More nervous than excited, but it felt the same.

"Kiss Peter? I'll try if you want me to," Sara said.

"You'd have to step over me first," I said, and turned up the radio loud.

The minute I saw Peter that night I knew our relationship had changed into something serious. When he wrapped the ribboned gardenia he brought around my wrist my head felt light and his fingers were warm on my wrist. We stood closer together than normal, we held hands, and our arms touched when we sat down. When Peter caught my eyes, even if he was only a few inches from me, I didn't feel nervous and look away like usual. I simply looked back into his dark eyes and wished I could put into words how I felt. And I could tell by the way he held me a few moments after the music ended on each slow dance that he was feeling close to me, too.

I saw Sara at the dance. She'd crashed it without a date with a bunch of people from the musical, which was very Sara-like. Even when she showed up somewhere with some poor guy who thought he was on a date, he was lucky to see her for more than a small part of the evening. Everyone liked to be around Sara and she shone in situations like this. She danced with a lot of other girls' dates and then in a big group with no one in particular. She and Anita had some steps down that they performed together while everyone formed a circle around them. I stiffened up and felt a lump in my throat.

"Let's join them," Peter said.

"What?!" He may as well have said we ought to perform a trapeze act.

"Come on, they're hogging the dance floor. Let's go!" he said, and pulled me through the crowd.

We were on the dance floor, Peter went up close to Sara and danced. This was a side of him I hadn't seen. I stood there like an idiot for a few seconds, and then realized I'd look stupider just standing still while my best friend and Peter and Anita danced. My arms and legs felt like lead, but I started moving. Peter grabbed both my hands and danced with me. Sara was smiling and laughing. She brushed past me and elbowed me in the ribs.

"That boyfriend of yours isn't half bad," she said, loud enough for Peter to hear.

"Hey, half bad, half good, depends on how you look at it," Peter said. We danced until we got sweaty and my dress seemed to be sticking to me, but I never felt tired.

The evening floated by, and I sent telepathic messages to the clock to try and slow it down. I couldn't get enough of being in Peter's arms, swaying to the music and feeling his cheek against my hair.

They announced the last song. When the bright lights came on, Peter draped his arms over my shoulders and pressed his forehead against mine.

"Thank you for inviting me, Amy. I was starting to think you were just humoring me, putting up with me at practice and school," he said. He was so close to me I could see the amber-colored lines in his dark brown eyes. "I've had a crush on you since the third grade."

"You sure took your time," I said.

"I was never brave enough to say anything. You are the pastor's daughter, after all," he said, and I knew by the way his eyes crinkled at the corners he was teasing.

"What's the real reason?" I asked.

"I don't know. . . . I guess when your mom . . . when you had that tragedy in your family, I was afraid. And then you stopped coming to church, and I didn't know what to do."

There it was. The old, dull pain that I carried around everywhere but had been almost able to forget, just for tonight. I took a deep breath and willed it to go away.

"Thank goodness for the chorus parts," I said, and tried to smile.

We walked out to Peter's ancient Oldsmobile Omega and he fought with the passenger side door to get it open. I got in and tried to figure out where to sit—on my side next to the door or in the middle next to Peter?

"Come on over next to me," Peter said, once he was in the car. I slid over next to him. His arm brushed mine as he turned the key and the engine sputtered and coughed before it finally started.

The night air was freezing and the heat didn't work, so we were chilled through. We pulled up to my house. All the lights were out, which meant Dad was already in bed. Earlier, I had worked out what I was going to say to get Peter to drop me off and not expect to come in. I didn't want to go in and have a big conversation with Dad, with him looking at me and winking at Peter and making a big scene. But now I wanted to think of something so Peter wouldn't go home right away. I wanted everything to stay exactly as it was. There was no other way to describe how good I felt except to say it was like someone had cast a spell over us and I didn't want to break it.

"Let me get the door for you," he said, and got out, which gave me a second to think.

He swung my door open, and let it hit the curb. He put out his hand to help me out of the car. He squeezed my hand tight and didn't let go until he had to use both hands to lift the car door up in place and jam it shut again.

"Do you want something to drink? I think there's some lemonade," I said.

"Sure," he said, and smiled big, so I knew he wanted to spend more time with me, because he couldn't possibly really want lemonade. We were both shaking from the cold. Lemonade sounded about as good as hot chocolate in a sauna. We went inside and Peter followed me into the kitchen.

"Sara sure was something out on the dance floor tonight, wasn't she?" Peter said. We were still shaking with cold. Dad hadn't thought to turn on the heat.

"She always is," I said. I was trying to get the lemonade out of the refrigerator without Peter seeing inside. When Dad was home he didn't pay attention much to things like the inside of the refrigerator, and cleaning wasn't exactly my forte, so it was an ugly sight. I was so grateful Sara had been over earlier and made lemonade. Otherwise, the only thing to offer Peter would have been the milk that Dad and I drink straight from the carton.

We sat down on the couch with our cold glasses and turned on the television. Some real-life cop show was on. The cops were on a high-speed chase, trying to catch a guy who'd just knifed someone at a restaurant.

"Howdy, howdy," hollered Dad, stomping down the stairs extra hard.

"Sorry to interrupt, but I forgot to turn on the dishwasher," he said, all smiles. He was wearing his white-and-red-striped pajamas and his hair was sticking up all over.

"The dishwasher is empty," I told him. He ignored me and stuck out his hand to Peter.

Peter hopped up and shook his hand like they were meeting for the first time.

"Hey ya, Peter. Good to see you. How was the dance?"

"The band was good; you know Mr. Luigi's son is the bass player—"

"It was great," I said, cutting Peter off. I made a face at Dad.

"Ah, yes, well . . . the dishwasher," he said, and went into the kitchen, but not before he winked at Peter. Dad clanged a few things around. Peter was still standing up, his hands shoved deep in his pockets.

"Good night, Peter. Good night, Amy. Don't stay up too late," Dad said, and went back upstairs.

"Your dad is the best," said Peter, and sat down.

"Yeah," I said. Dad's interruption made me tense.

The high-speed chase on the cop show had apparently ended. The paramedics were pulling someone out of a mangled car. I closed my eyes. I still couldn't handle car wrecks, or even the sound of an ambulance. Why hadn't my mother passed away quietly in a hospital somewhere? Would that have made it easier?

"Everyone's surprised how well he's done after your mom's accident," Peter said.

My mom's accident. My mom's death.

"He's not doing well," I snapped. "He drifts around in a fog. He spends all his time at church, and when he's not there, he's sleeping." I was getting worked up. I'd never said this out loud before. "He thinks if he works himself into the ground, serving everyone else, he'll just forget or something."

"Amy, I'm sorry, I didn't realize . . . ," Peter said.

"Yeah, well, no one realizes. He's doing a good put-on-a-happy-face show."

"Man, I'm sorry. I didn't mean to upset you." He grabbed both my hands in between his and gently warmed my icy fingertips.

"Sometimes I don't say the right thing, Amy, or like now, I don't know what to say at all. I just care a lot about your dad. And you."

My heart was pounding blood directly to my face. Now I was the one who didn't know what to say.

Peter got up to change the channel and then came back and sat next to me close, so close that he had to put his arm around my shoulders, so I knew he wasn't mad. Every part of me that was touching him was electrified. I tried to calm down. I liked Peter so close, but I didn't know what to do, where to look, so I stared straight ahead at the television and tried to look absorbed in the program. Nothing made sense. Not the TV program, not the way the thought of kissing Peter made me want to cry, like it would open up a wound in my insides I wouldn't be able to fix.

"Amy," Peter said, almost in a whisper.

I turned to look at him halfway. He put his hand on my cheek and moved my face toward his. I don't know why I did what I did next. I ducked my head down into his chest and put my hand on his opposite shoulder, like an awkward hug. He held still for a minute and then moved away from me so I had to look at him again. He didn't seem upset, so I figured everything was all right, except for how angry I was at myself. But he wasn't looking into my eyes anymore like he had been all night.

"I guess I should be going," he said softly.

"I had a good time tonight. Really, I mean it," I said.

"Thank you."

He stood up and put on his jacket. We walked to the door together. I opened it for him, and the cold air that blasted in made my eyes water.

"Thanks for the lemonade, Amy," he said, and zipped his coat collar up to his nose.

I watched him walk to his car and heave the door open and then shut. I wanted to scream at him to come back, that I didn't mean to make him go away, but instead I ran upstairs, unzipping my dress as I went. I slung it off my shoulders and left it in a pile by the side of my bed, crawled under the covers, and pulled them up over my head.

Chapter 15

MONDAY AFTER SCHOOL I found Sara in the auditorium where we were meeting to return costumes, music, and props from the musical. She sat at a table talking with Anita and some of the other people who played main parts, including Sandra.

"I saw you at the dance on Saturday," Sandra said.

"I didn't see you," I said, hoping to sound unfriendly enough that she'd leave me alone. But she was undeterred.

"You know," she said, "we sure miss you at church. You ought to come out again. We have a really great teacher for scripture class, and your dad *is* the pastor, after all."

I ignored her but she kept right on.

"I mean, I'm sure he'd be thrilled if he looked out over the pulpit and saw you sitting there in the congregation. He seems so sad all the time."

"You don't know anything about me or my dad," I told her. Who did she think she was?

"Amy, you know I don't want to overstep my bounds or anything, but it's true that we all miss you, especially your dad. You can see it in his face." She leaned over and put her hand over mine. I wanted to scratch her eyes out. I pulled my hand away from hers.

"Peter seems to be the only one able to get through to you, Amy. I wish you'd let the rest of us help you, too."

I would have stood up and slapped her that very second if I hadn't felt two hands come down on my shoulders and inhaled Peter's clean-soap smell. I tensed and didn't move. I was angry. Angry at Sandra, I guess, but really angry at Peter. Was I his idea of someone who needed his *help*?

"Whoa, Amy, loosen those shoulders," he said. "Mr. Alberts wants the chorus people to come over to the gym. Want to walk over with me?"

Suddenly, hearing Peter's voice and feeling his hands massage my tight muscles made my anger disappear. He couldn't really think of me as a loser who needed him. I glared at Sandra and stood up.

"Bye, Sara," I said over her head. "See you later."

Sara looked up, surprised. She hadn't realized I was sitting there. "Yeah, sure, Amy. See ya." Anita waved at me and pulled her chair closer to Sara. She whispered something in her ear that made Sara look at me and raise her eyebrows.

I walked away with Peter, especially close to him so he was practically forced to put his arm around me. I desperately needed to believe that Peter wanted to be with me for reasons he couldn't explain. Reasons that actually went against what was comfortable and easy. Reasons like mine for being with him.

That night, I made a poached egg and poured maple syrup over the top. It was something Mom always did when she was hungry late at night. She'd sit and talk to me, but mostly she'd just listen, and sometimes we'd fall asleep on the couch. The next morning the egg and syrup would be dried hard on the plate and she'd have to scrub it off with a Brillo pad. I didn't really like the salty-sweet combination, but I needed to feel close to her tonight, and I didn't know how else to do it. Houdini made himself comfortable in my lap and purred.

I sat licking the syrup mixed with the runny yellow yolk off my fork and tried to imagine what Mom would say about what Sandra said. Even with my eyes shut tight and concentrating as hard as I could, I couldn't figure out anything. Maybe because Mom wouldn't even know me now. When she disappeared from my life she took that part of my insides that made me believe in good things and gave me a reason to get out of bed in the morning.

"Amy, I didn't know you were home." Dad startled me. He walked down the stairs in his old robe and a big red mark up one side of his face where he'd been sleeping on it.

"I didn't know you were here either," I said.

"I fell asleep on my books at my desk," he said, and rubbed at the red mark. I wondered if he would notice what I was eating.

"How are things going with you and Sara?" he asked. What a strange question. He came over and scratched Houdini's ears.

"Why?"

"I'm just wondering, that's all," he said.

"Fine. Why wouldn't things be okay?"

He looked at me for a long time and then finally noticed the plate in my hand.

"I thought I smelled something familiar," he said with a sad kind of smile. "We used to make fun of her for eating that."

"I know," I said. Suddenly I felt really embarrassed and didn't like the emotion that was between us. Just a few minutes ago I'd been trying to invite my mom's presence and now I wanted it away, tucked back into places where it didn't hurt so much.

"You didn't answer me," I said. "Why wouldn't things be okay with Sara?" I tried not to sound defensive, even though that's how I felt. I let Houdini lick the leftover egg off my plate.

"Oh, I don't know. No reason," he said, and went into the kitchen.

Chapter 16

PETER KNEW THAT Sara and I were together every Friday night, so when he didn't call me Friday after school, I was a little disappointed, but not surprised. And, after all, I was looking forward to seeing a new movie with her.

I went into the kitchen and rummaged around looking for something to eat. There was a bag of popcorn kernels behind the box of stale soda crackers that I couldn't remember buying. They must have been more than a year old. I figured popcorn didn't get stale, as long as it was in the kernel, so I heated some oil in the frying pan and threw in a handful. Since I hated the movie theater popcorn, I threw in some extra to bring for me and Sara. I guess I put in way too much, because it started popping all over the place. I ran to get a lid, but ended up using it as a shield against the hot flying popcorn.

The phone rang. I picked it up, popcorn still zinging off the pot lid, expecting to hear Sara's voice.

"Amy?" It was Dorothy. "How's it going, hon?"

"Fine, except for a catastrophe in the kitchen," I said. She laughed.

"Tell me about it. Say, can I talk to Sara? She's got my checkbook."

"Sara's not here," I said. "Maybe she's on her way over."

"Hmmm. I thought she said she was going to your house, but that was a while ago. Oh, well, I probably wasn't listening," Dorothy said. "What's that noise?"

"Popcorn for the movie," I said. "I'll probably see Sara in a few hours. If she hasn't got in touch with you by then, should I give her a message?"

"Yeah, tell her to hustle her buns home with my checkbook!" Dorothy said.

It occurred to me that Sara and I hadn't actually made plans, or even mentioned going out tonight. Or had we talked about tonight and I'd forgotten? I didn't think so. By the time I cleaned up the kitchen and got the popcorn that hadn't fallen on the floor into a bag, it was dinnertime. I dialed Sara's number to see if Dorothy had heard from her, but no one answered.

I sat in the living room trying to outguess the *Wheel of Fortune* contestants and munching on the popcorn. Then, halfway through *Jeopardy*, I rang Sara again. This time Dorothy answered.

"Sara was just here," she said. I'd obviously woken her up. "I know because my checkbook's here with a note. 'Gone to the movies.'" There was a long pause as Dorothy yawned. "So I guess she's at the movies."

"Thanks," I said, and hung up, confused.

I decided to walk over to the theater. At least a movie would be a distraction, even if I couldn't find Sara there. I walked slow, because it was cold and the unusually dry air stung my cheeks and lips. I stopped in front of Finnegan's Drugstore where there was light and searched in my pocket for lip balm.

Someone walked up close to me and for a second I hoped it might be Peter. But it was Ray, a knit cap pulled down low over his ears. His breath came out in little puffs.

"Where you headed?" he asked me.

"To the movies," I said.

"Alone?"

"Yeah, alone," I said.

"Me, too. Let's walk over together," he said.

"Sara's probably there," I said, curious about his reaction.

"Hmmmm," he said. He was poker-faced.

By the time we got there, the theater was packed and it was hard to see through the crowds. Ray and I bought our tickets to a new sci-fi movie and went inside, up on the raised platform where they have the video games. Ray watched some kid play who didn't look old enough to be here without his parents, and I scanned the crowd for Sara. I didn't see her, so I stood by Ray and watched the boy at the video game, racking up points by the hundreds of thousands.

I decided to get myself a drink, so I turned and headed toward the concession booth. There was Sara, her back toward me, standing in line. Right before I tapped her on the shoulder, I saw Anita. I'd thought when the musical ended, she'd go away or something. She stood in front of Sara, close to her, laughing loudly at everything she said. I glanced down and thought I saw their fingers entwined. Sara put her hand on Anita's arm and held it there a long time. Way too long. Now I was sure they were holding hands, between themselves where it was hard to see, like they were hiding it. Anita turned to whisper something in Sara's ear and saw me.

"Hey, Amy," said Anita, and she quickly let go of Sara's hand. The wind went out of me like I'd been punched in the stomach.

Sara whirled around. "Amy! Hi!"

"Hi," I said, keeping my eyes down. I studied the yellow Styrofoam-like popcorn littering the floor.

"I hoped, I mean, thought you'd be with Peter. . . ." Sara said.

"Uh, you want to join us?" asked Anita.

I looked up. Sara had a tight smile on her face.

"No, I came with my friend," I said. Sara knew I was lying, even though it wasn't really a lie. Ray was a friend, wasn't he? Her smile lost its tight look.

"She's in the bathroom right now," I said. I didn't want to bring up Ray. "I better go find her. Movie's about to start."

I walked as casually as I could to the bathroom, but couldn't breathe.

I swung open the door to a stall and locked it. Hot liquid gathered in my throat. Then I sat on the closed lid of the toilet, shut my eyes tight, and willed myself not to throw up.

"Amy? Amy?" Sara's voice.

I pulled my knees up to my chest so my feet wouldn't show. My face was sweating and a powerful wave of nausea swept over me. I squeezed my eyes shut tighter and held my breath. I didn't want to see Sara. I wanted her to go away.

"Amy, I know you're in here," she said. A toilet flushed and some lady in clicking heels walked out, not stopping to wash her hands.

Anita and Sara. Sara and Anita.

I heard Sara move along the stalls, stopping in front of each one.

"Excuse me," someone said.

"Sorry," said Sara. She must have been peeking between the crack of each closed door. I didn't care if Sara knew exactly where I was. I wasn't moving.

"Amy, listen to me. Please come out," Sara said. Her voice sounded different than normal, like she was afraid.

I knew every intonation of her voice, everything about her. At least I'd thought I did.

The door swung open and a bunch of loud girls began banging doors, running water, laughing and shouting. After they left I listened for a long time to make sure Sara was gone. I slowly unbent my legs and took three deep breaths. The nausea had gone, but the pain that settled in the pit of my stomach was getting worse.

Terrible feelings swam around in my gut and made my head dizzy. They all kind of mixed together into one overwhelming thing. Sara had abandoned me. Or the person I thought was Sara.

Chapter 17

THE PHONE RANG AND RANG. Finally I turned the ringer off. I sat and stared at the caller ID with Sara's number listed about a dozen times. She didn't leave any messages. Then another number came up that I didn't recognize. I glanced at the clock—12:30 A.M.

"Hello?"

"What happened to you?" Ray said. "You were standing right next to me and then you were gone. I looked all over."

"I'm sorry," I said. "I got sick all of a sudden and had to come home."

"Are you all right now?"

"Not really," I said. "Hey, you know that argument you and Sara got into when you asked her to your homecoming?"

"It wasn't an argument," Ray said. "Not exactly."

"What was it then?"

"I'm not sure. She made it clear she's not interested in me. Not now, not ever. It hurt my feelings pretty bad. I accused her of some things, and it got kind of uncomfortable. But like I said, it wasn't really an argument. I just don't understand her, I guess."

"I don't think I do either," I said.

"That's odd coming from you. I thought you two were as close as two people could get," he said.

"I thought we were, too." I said, then a shiver ran up my spine. Were we too close? Is that why I hated Anita?

"I've gotta go," I told Ray. "I'll talk to you later." I hung up quick, even though he was trying to say something else.

My head felt heavy on the pillow as I thought about Sara. I'd do anything for her. I loved Sara. But those feelings were different than what I felt for Peter, I was positive. I stared at the caller ID again for a while, but no one else called.

I needed to talk to someone about this, but I wasn't sure I could put into words what I felt, or even what was actually happening. And who could I confide in? Not Ray, not Dad, definitely not Peter. What would Peter say if he knew?

The front door opened and startled me. Then I heard Dad talking to Houdini in the hall. I pretended I was asleep until he went upstairs, taking the cat with him. Finally, after it was still, I went upstairs, too, and curled up in a ball under my covers. I played sick the rest of the weekend, which wasn't far from the truth. I didn't answer the phone for Sara or Peter, or even Dad when he called. My brain shut down. I didn't think much, even though I couldn't sleep. The only thing I could do was keep my eyes shut and wish this would all go away.

On Monday I went to school, hoping this was all a big mistake. I shouldn't have come. It felt like everyone knew about Sara and Anita. Every conversation before and after class and in the hallways was hushed, it seemed, and stopped anytime I got near. I didn't know how everyone knew so quickly. Or was it only my imagination?

I left my class before lunch a little early. I just got up and left. The teacher didn't say anything. I couldn't face Sara at lunch, I couldn't stand all the little circles of people speculating and looking at me and talking about Sara and Anita. This was like the time Geoff Hill and Kim Lee were rumored to have slept together in the seventh grade. No one really knew if it was true, but that didn't stop us all from staring and talking and thinking about it. I went to the vending machine in the cafeteria to buy a Coke. The machine wouldn't take the crumpled-up dollar I found in my pocket, so I had to dig around in my backpack for change.

The bell rang and I tried to get out of there before everyone came in, but I didn't make it. I was fighting the crowd, going the wrong way, as everyone poured into the cafeteria. I got out one door just as Sara and Anita were about to go in through the other. They looked happy. Was Sara happy?

I walked quickly, intending to go home, but ended up on Sara's doorstep instead. I rang the bell and waited. Dorothy was probably still in bed, so I rang it again a couple of times.

"Just a minute. Hang on," I heard her say out her bedroom window.

This might be a mistake. Maybe Dorothy didn't even know. But then again, maybe she could explain a few things.

The door flew open and Dorothy stood there blinking in the light.

"Amy, come in, come in," she said. "What are you doing here? Isn't it time for school yet?"

"Actually it's lunch. I need to talk to you," I said.

"Let me get some coffee first. I can't function until I've had some coffee." She waved her hand toward the couch and I sat down and waited.

"So . . ." She sat down, sipped her coffee, and waited for me to speak.

"I want to talk to you about Sara . . . ," I said, not sure where to start.

"You two have a fight?" she asked.

"No, no. It's just that . . . do you know her friend Anita?"

"Ah," she said, and put her cup down.

"I saw them at the movies on Friday. They were . . . they were holding hands," I said. "Really holding hands."

Dorothy held up her hand in front of my face and exhaled with a long whistling sound. "I thought they were going to keep their relationship private."

"Relationship?" I asked. I wanted Dorothy to tell me I had it all wrong. Dorothy raised one eyebrow, but didn't answer.

"But when . . . ," I began.

"It's been a while," she said. "She didn't want you to know. Or me."

"But you *did* know!" I was surprised Sara would tell Dorothy something like this before me. "Why didn't she tell me when she told you?"

"She didn't. I found out the hard way, like you."

"How?"

"I don't want to talk about it. Don't want to know about it or hear about it. Me and Sara haven't been talking much lately." Dorothy took a long drink of coffee and a long look at me. "This hurts me, too."

"Have you known for long?" I asked.

"A few months. I'm trying to understand. I've even tried a little religion. Or at least as much as I could take. Your dad makes it go down easy. Sort of like medicine with a spoonful of sugar."

I considered this for a minute. That explained the envelope I found in Dorothy's purse. "But Dad wouldn't approve . . . of Sara and Anita."

"Not of their relationship. But he does approve of unconditional love, right?"

"I guess so," I said. I wasn't sure of anything at the moment. Dad knew, too?

"Actually, I'm not quite sure why I would lean on a preacher, of all things. Part of it, maybe, was worrying about you and your friendship with Sara. She was afraid you wouldn't be her friend anymore."

"Why would she think that?" I asked.

"Maybe because I had such a hard time. She didn't think I loved her anymore, for a while." Dorothy pinched her lips together, remembering.

"Another reason, I'm sure, are your religious beliefs."

"Oh," I said. I thought about this. It was funny that Sara was considering my beliefs a part of this whole equation, given that I hadn't believed in anything for a long time.

"Don't get bent out of shape at Sara for not telling you. I didn't deal very well when I found out." Dorothy lit a cigarette and took a long drag. "So everyone knows?"

"I'm not sure. I think some do."

"She's going to need you," Dorothy said. "It's guaranteed some of the other kids will be nasty to her."

"I don't think you need to worry about that," I said. "Sara can hold her own."

Could I?

Chapter 18

I AVOIDED SARA, school, and even Peter for the next week. I wondered what Peter was thinking about me, I mean about Sara and me and the fact that I didn't want to kiss him that night of the homecoming dance. During the day, I sat home with Houdini on my lap and slept as much as he did. After school the phone would ring and Sara and Peter and the school secretary would leave messages. I simply listened to them, lacking the energy to pick up the phone. A few times, someone would knock on the door, but I'd pretend no one was home.

Before Dad came home, I'd throw my coat on the floor and spread some schoolbooks around and erase the messages on the machine so he wouldn't worry. Not that he would notice anything was wrong. The days went by so slow they were unbearable. By Thursday I couldn't take it anymore. I couldn't take another nap or sit on the couch one more day, but I didn't want to go to school and see Sara or Peter either.

The phone rang as I was leaving for the grocery store for some cat food and I picked it up. By accident.

"Amy? Is that you? This is Ms. Newman."

"Hi," I said, embarrassed I hadn't been to class, but not as much as I should have been. Everything seemed a bit foggy lately, like it wasn't real.

"Is anything wrong? No one's been able to get in touch with you, and Sara's been a complete mess," she said.

"I'm sorry I haven't been there to help," I said, not wanting to go into it.

"You're such a good student. I'd hate to see you blow it over a fight with a friend. Or whatever it is," Ms. Newman said. I stayed silent.

"So when do you plan to come back?" she finally asked.

Even if I wanted to say anything, I couldn't because the words would have stuck in my throat.

"If you don't come back, I'm not going to have any choice but to give you no credit for the period you're supposed to be my teacher's aide. I imagine the same is happening in your other classes."

Somehow I had convinced myself the fog really would lift and I'd be able to start over, like none of this ever happened. But with Ms. Newman telling me this on the phone, it was all too real all of a sudden.

"Amy? Are you still there?"

"I'm here," I said.

"You're one of my best students. That's why I'm concerned. I know it's been a rough year . . . you made it through your mother's death. You can make it through this," she said.

"Through what?" I didn't think Ms. Newman knew, or she wouldn't wonder why I wasn't at school.

"Finding out Sara's gay."

I made a small croaking sound, cleared my throat and said, "Thank you for calling. I'll be okay." Then I hung up. The word *gay* came out like it had a capital G and an exclamation point, even though Ms. Newman's voice hadn't changed at all. For some reason I couldn't say it or even think it yet. I was upset Ms. Newman said it out loud. There was a whole lot more to Sara than being gay. I hated the label and how it might attach itself like a neon sign that no one would see her through.

Besides that, I didn't "make it through" any-thing. Making it through meant I came out on the other side of something and left the blackness behind.

I went to school the next day. I kept to myself as much as possible, but ended up in a study group with Sara in the library for phys ed, of all things.

I tried avoiding eye contact with Sara. I couldn't concentrate. The words were blurry. I couldn't think. Sara's book stayed open on the same page for a long time before she finally said something.

"Amy? I'm sorry," she said.

I kept quiet.

"I'm sorry I hurt you." I looked up and her eyes were all watery and red. "You're my best friend."

"How can you say that?" I hissed.

"Because it's true!"

"I'll bet Anita wouldn't agree," I said.

We both went back to our books for a little while, but she wasn't reading. The other kids at the table didn't seem to be either. They kept looking up at me and Sara to see what would happen next, I guess.

"Amy, look, you can be mad at me. I'm mad at myself for not telling you earlier. I just didn't know how to tell you, or what your reaction would be. I did what I thought was best, and I made a mistake, okay? Be mad at me if you want, but why ruin your relationship with Peter? *I* screwed up here, not him," Sara said.

"It's stupid," I said. "You wouldn't understand, anyway."

"What makes you think I wouldn't understand?"

She did understand me, always. Sara seemed like herself; what had I expected? That she would suddenly grow a tail or turn purple? It felt like it was me who was changed.

"And anyway, what makes you think anything is wrong with my relationship with Peter?"

"I've been talking to him. He said you acted weird after the dance. He said you guys had a great time and then you wouldn't let him kiss you. And now you won't talk to him."

This disturbed me a little, Sara and Peter discussing me, but I was too tired to get upset about it. I'd think about it later, I decided. It felt good to talk to Sara again. I took a deep breath.

"I don't know why I acted like that after the dance," I said. "But the rest is your fault. I don't know what he thinks of me now."

Sara's face flushed a little and she shifted in her seat. "No one thinks . . . no one has any reason to think anything about you," she said.

"You don't know that," I said.

"I know Peter's not worried about it," Sara said. "I cleared that up with him right away."

"Thank you *so* much," I said, mean enough to make Sara look away. We stared back down at our books.

"I can't stand it when you get like this."

"Like what? I didn't ask for this."

"I'm sorry, really, really sorry. But there's no reason to pull away from everything that could make you happy. You act like you don't deserve anything good. Like you have to wallow in unhappiness all the time."

I slapped my book shut and shoved my papers in my bag. The chair squeaked loudly when I slid it back, and a bunch of people at the next table looked over.

"Sit down, Amy," Sara said, real low.

"Has it occurred to you that I *am* unhappy all the time?" I asked.

"You don't have to be. It's not required. No one's going to think you didn't love your mom if you don't go around moping all the time," she said.

"What does this conversation have to do with my mom? You have no idea what you're talking about. You don't understand anything about losing someone you love." I was talking loud now, trying to hold my shaky voice steady.

Sara stared at me hard. "I'm losing you, aren't I?"

Someone at the other table laughed. Someone else made kissing noises. For once I didn't care. Let them think whatever they wanted.

"It's not the same," I said. "And in case you need to be reminded, you're the one that's ruined our friendship. You spend all your time with Anita. How am I supposed to compete with your *girlfriend*?" I put on my backpack and left her there.

"I can't prop you up forever, Amy! You need to stand on your own two feet!" She shouted this across the room, but she may as well have slapped me across the face.

I slammed the door on the whooping and laughing. My insides were hurting and my brain felt wrung out, so I walked home, not caring that I was going to flunk out.

Chapter 19

THE NEXT MORNING, Dad was milling around the kitchen in his beat-up robe, looking lost.

"What are you looking for?" I asked. I had no intention of going to school, so I hoped he would leave soon. I was already half an hour late.

"I just got a hankering for some oatmeal. But I can't find any," he said.

"This is a new thing," I said, "you wanting breakfast."

"I just woke up and wanted oatmeal," he said, and shrugged his shoulders. I noticed how skinny he was, like his robe was draped over one of those wire dummies you see in department stores.

"Let me see if I can find some," I said, and set my glass of orange juice on the counter. I rummaged through the cupboards and came up with a package of cinnamon-apple instant oatmeal. The expiration date was last month, but I figured it wouldn't hurt to make it anyway. Dad sat down at the table and watched me heat up some water in the microwave and mix it into a bowl with the oatmeal. He had large dark circles under his eyes and he hadn't shaved, but something in his face made him seem a lot more awake than I'd seen him in a long time.

I plopped the oatmeal and a spoon down in front of him. Then I poured him some orange juice out of my glass, because it was all that was left.

He took two bites of oatmeal and then a big tear dripped out of the corner of his eye and rolled down to his chin. It hung on the tip for a second and then dropped into the oatmeal. He stirred the oatmeal around and kept eating, not caring about all the crying that was going into his bowl.

"Dad?" I said.

He kept eating until he scraped the bowl clean and washed it down with the orange juice. Then he leaned back in the chair and let the tears roll down his chin and neck and into his robe.

"Dad?" I said again.

"I'm sorry. Sometimes I just . . . I can't . . ." He put his hand over his face and his whole body shook.

He looked like a little kid, but really old at the same time. I put my hand against my chest because it felt like my heart was going to rip right out if I didn't hold it in. I wanted to run away, as fast as I could.

I put my hand on the doorknob and twisted it, thinking I could hurry and make it to my second class, but I didn't open the door. I had no idea what to do or what to say but I stayed. I watched him cry for a while because he had so much stored up.

Finally, when he started hiccuping like a baby, I went into the bathroom and brought him some tissues and a damp washcloth.

"Here, Dad," I said, and he looked up at me surprised. I guess he'd forgotten I was there. He washed off his face and pulled himself together a little.

Houdini jumped up on the table to see if there were any leftovers. Dad scratched his ears.

"Getting this cat was a good thing, I think," he said.

"He's attached to you," I said. Houdini actually preferred Dad to me, even though I was the one who took care of him.

Dad looked at me, not blinking. "Why aren't you in school?" he asked.

I tried to think of an excuse. Finally, I just shrugged my shoulders. His hiccuping from the crying spell died down and he relaxed a little.

"You want to take a drive?"

I nodded my head. Taking a drive was something our family used to do. I don't even think I'd been in a car with Dad for more than a few minutes lately. A drive sounded like just the thing we both needed.

When Dad emerged from his room a while later, he looked good except that his eyes were still red.

"Should we take Houdini?" I asked.

"Why not?" he said.

We packed a lunch, including a can of tuna for the cat, from what we could rummage from the kitchen. A few drink boxes, a bag of peeled carrots that didn't look too old, a box of crackers, some cheese, and candy bars. I remembered the can opener and some napkins last.

We drove north, out of the city and toward Bellingham, Mom's favorite place to visit on Sundays after church. Houdini yowled the first fifteen minutes solid and dug his claws into the upholstery. Then he hid under the seat and closed his eyes. Dad and I were quiet, not needing to say anything, and not uncomfortable with the silence for once. After an hour flew by, Dad pulled into a gas station with a Quickie Mart attached.

"I need to make a pit stop," he said. "I'm going to get some painkiller, too. My shoulder feels stiff. Why don't you take the cat to that area over there and see if he needs to go." Dad pointed to a vacant field next to the gas station.

I pulled Houdini out from under the seat and walked with him tucked under my arm to the field. When I set him down, he went all wiggly and wouldn't let me put him down. He wasn't used to being outside.

"Come on, Houdini," I coaxed. I sat down, showing him it was all right and let him sit on my lap. I held very still and waited until he relaxed a little, stuck his neck over my ankles, and started to nibble on the long grass. I closed my eyes and turned my face up to the sun. Dad was taking a long time. The air was cold, but I could feel the sun's warmth if I concentrated. I pushed Sara to the back of my mind. It felt good to be away.

A siren startled me and Houdini clawed my leg.

"Ouch!" I picked him up and looked over to the ambulance screeching into the parking lot. The paramedics jumped out and ran into the Quickie Mart. I sat and watched, wondering what was going on. Dad would be comforting whoever was in trouble. So when they brought him out on the stretcher, I didn't believe it for a second. Then I ran toward the ambulance, my vision tunneled, my feet barely touching the ground, moving in slow motion. I didn't breathe, and the only sound was my heart pounding in my ears.

Chapter 20

I KNEW THAT Dad was all right when they let me in to see him right away when I got to the hospital, but adrenaline still rushed through my body and my heart wouldn't slow down. They hustled me out quick, but Dad was conscious and even smiled at me.

While we waited, an admissions clerk let Houdini sit under his desk inside an empty, turned-over mesh wastebasket, even though it was against the rules. But Houdini started yowling and I had to take him out and leave him in the car. I opened the tuna fish and set it out on some napkins. I cracked the window open a bit.

"I'll be back soon," I said. Houdini attacked the tuna fish and didn't pay any attention when I left.

A nurse was looking for me when I came back in. "Your dad had what we think is an anxiety attack. There's nothing wrong with his heart, and we can't find anything else. He's going to be all right," he said. "The doctor will be out in a minute."

"Thanks," I said. I paced around the waiting room, relieved, but still antsy. I wanted Mom. I wanted Sara.

The nurse came back out and said I could go and see Dad again. Dad was out of it, and a nurse hovered over him. I squeezed his hand. When another nurse came in to check his IV, I went back out to the waiting room until the doctor came to find me.

"We can't find anything wrong, physically, but we'll keep him overnight for tests and observation. From speaking with your father, I believe it was acute anxiety," the doctor said. "I think your dad will be just fine. He'll need plenty of rest, though, when you go home and I'll recommend counseling once we've ruled out physical causes. I understand it's just you and him?"

"Yes," I said. "And a cat."

The doctor smiled. He had a gap between his front teeth, but they were perfectly white and straight. "Well, then. Are there friends or other family who can help out for a while?"

It occurred to me I ought to let someone at the church know what happened. "My dad's a pastor," I said. "We'll probably have a refrigerator full of casseroles by the time we get home." The doctor laughed. He really did have a nice smile—it was genuine.

So when the same doctor came out to the waiting room and told me I ought to go home and rest myself, I trusted him.

"Can I see Dad again before I leave?" I asked.

"He's asleep, but you can peek in. Follow me."

I looked in at Dad through the half-open door. His skin seemed a little gray, but he slept peacefully.

"Are you sure he's going to be all right?"

"Don't you worry. We'll take care of him," the doctor said. I started crying a little, right then, from relief and exhaustion and because the doctor was so kind to me.

"Thank you. You'll tell him I was here?"

"Of course," he said.

When I opened the car door, a really disgusting smell hit me.

"Houdini, you didn't!" I said. But of course he had. What did I expect? I gathered up the tuna-oil-soaked napkins and cleaned up the mess the best I could. At least it was in the backseat. I rolled down all the windows and drove home, shaking and covered with goose bumps. All I could think about was getting to Sara's.

I parked the car outside Sara's house and hesitated a minute before getting out. When I finally knocked, no one answered. Could my luck be any worse? I closed the car door and rested my head on the steering wheel. Could I be any more alone? I wanted to sit there and feel sorry for myself, but I just felt tired. I was tired beyond exhaustion. Tired beyond needing sleep.

"Let's get you home," I told the cat.

The first thing I noticed when we got home was Dad's oatmeal bowl still on the table. I brought it to the sink and turned on the water to soak it. I glanced at the caller ID, expecting to see Sara's or Peter's number, but there was nothing. Maybe they'd both given up on me. I picked up the phone and called Peter before I could talk myself out of it. He answered.

"Can you come over?" I asked. There was a long pause.

"I'll be right there," he said.

It seemed an eternity, but finally, he knocked on the door.

"Hi, Amy," Peter said. He stood with his hands in his pockets, his shoulders tensed, and his hair fallen over one eye. He brushed it back.

"My dad's in the hospital." I hadn't thought to say anything else. Maybe I should have started with "Hello."

"What?" Peter looked panicked.

"He's going to be okay. The doctor said so. He's just been under a lot of pressure."

Peter stepped inside and put one hand on my arm.

"Are you okay?" he asked.

"Sort of," I said. "This scared me." Peter led me over to the couch and we sat down.

"I've been worried about you," Peter said. "I didn't know about your dad . . . I've been worried why you wouldn't answer my calls or come to school . . . Sara said it isn't about me . . . I know what's going on . . . ," he broke off and cleared his throat. "But we can talk about that stuff another time. Can I do anything to help you?"

"Would you find Sara for me? Tell her I need her?"

"Yeah, I can do that," he said. "I'm here, too."

"We have a lot to talk about," I said.

"Yes, we do. But for now I'm going to go get Sara."

"Thanks," I said.

When he left, I laid down on the couch, pulled a blanket up to my chin, and waited for Sara.

When I woke up, I felt like I'd been asleep for hours and hours, but I could see light through the cracks in the window blinds. I wondered why Sara hadn't come yet. I clicked on the television. A morning program was on. The temperature and time were posted in the corner of the screen—7:55 A.M. I'd slept all night! I forgot about Sara and ran to call the hospital. I hoped Dad wasn't wondering where I was. I didn't want him to feel alone.

The receptionist put me right through to Dad's room. He wasn't in emergency anymore. An unfamiliar voice answered the phone.

"Is my dad there?" I asked.

"Is this Amy?" the voice asked.

"Yes."

"Hang on a second." I heard my dad talking in the background. Someone laughed.

"Amy, how are you?" Dad asked.

"The question is, how are you? Who's there with you?"

"I'm feeling good. Rick is here from the church."

"Oh, of course," I said. Peter would have told everyone.

"I must have scared you," Dad said. "Sorry we didn't get to finish our drive."

"Were you afraid?" I asked.

"No, not for myself," he said. "I could only think

146

about what a rotten thing this would be to pull on you."

"I'll get dressed and come up right away," I said. I looked down at myself. Actually I was still dressed from yesterday. A little crumpled, but dressed.

"You don't need to," he said. "I'm really okay. The doctor even says I'll be able to go home soon. I feel like I ought to."

"You don't want me to come?" I asked, hurt.

"That's not it at all. Like I said, I feel bad about scaring you, and I want you to take care of yourself."

"I am," I said. "But you have to promise to do the same."

"I've been burning the candle at both ends, haven't I?" he said.

"Yeah."

"I changed my mind about what I said earlier. I don't want you to take care of yourself. I want to take care of you from now on," he said. "I'm going to be home more. The Lord will take care of what I can't."

I smiled into the phone. I remembered Dad saying this same thing to Mom in the evenings when he'd turn the ringer off the phone and spend time with us, playing a game or watching TV.

"We'll take care of each other," I said. I barely recognized the light feeling inside my body. Maybe things were starting to look up.

Chapter 21

SARA AND PETER CAME OVER about an hour after my dad got home that afternoon. He'd just gone to sleep in his bed when they knocked on the door.

I'd been rushing around cleaning up the house and doing laundry. I even attempted to make some food in case Dad got hungry—macaroni and cheese out of a box. I threw in some frozen peas so it would be halfway healthy and stuck it in the refrigerator.

"Do I smell food?" Sara asked. It felt good to have her here, but both of us kept some distance. Things weren't quite back to normal. I was still smarting over her last words to me.

"Macaroni. I thought Dad might get hungry," I said. "But I made a ton. Want some? Peter?"

"Sure," they said at the same time. I wasn't convinced they really wanted it or if they just didn't want to hurt my feelings by saying no.

"We came in last night," Sara said. "You were asleep, and we didn't want to wake you."

I dished out three bowls and thought about Sara and Peter looking at me while I was asleep. I hope I don't snore. I stuck the bowls in the microwave. We sat in an uncomfortable silence while the microwave ticked off the time, but still it felt better than being alone, even with Dad in his room. When the timer beeped, Sara grabbed some hot pads and helped me set the bowls on the table.

Peter made small talk about people at school while we ate. The noodles were mushy and the peas were still a little cold on the inside. Finally Sara put down her fork and looked straight at me.

"Can you forgive me for keeping my secret from you?" she said. Peter looked from me to her and shoveled some macaroni in his mouth.

I didn't know what to say. And then I didn't have to say anything, because someone knocked at the door. I shot up from my seat and went to answer it. Sandra and the old group that used to come every Monday afternoon stood on the doorstep.

"We brought your dad some balloons," Sandra said. One of the other girls held on to a bunch of balloons, with a Mylar one in the middle that said "Get Well" and had a goofy clown face on it. "And something for you." She handed me a card. It said "Amy" in loopy writing with daisies all over it. Back to being a charity project.

"Thanks," I said. "Dad's resting right now."

"It's okay," Sandra said. "We weren't planning on staying. Just wanted to let you know we were thinking about you."

"Thanks, that's really nice," I said.

"Call us if you need anything."

"Sure," I said. A cold day in hell, I thought.

They shuffled away and Sara came up behind me.

"Church people?" she asked.

"Yeah."

"Nice balloons," she said, smiling.

"I hate clowns," I said.

"Yeah, well, they're for your dad."

"I'll bring them up later. I don't want to wake him up."

"You didn't answer my question," Sara said. "Can you forgive me?"

"I can't deal with this right now," I said. "I've got my dad to worry about."

Sara bit her lip, looked at the floor, and didn't say anything.

Peter walked in, wiping his face with his sleeve.

"Did I hear Sandra?"

Sara answered for me. "Yeah. They brought a clown balloon. Hey, we should go now."

Peter turned to me. "You take care of yourself. I'll call you later. If you want me to."

"That would be nice," I said.

I heard Dad moving around upstairs so I brought the balloons up. I opened the door to his room and pulled the oversize bundle inside. Houdini leaped off the bed and hid underneath. Dad stood by his dresser, slipping on his watch. He looked good.

"What's this?"

"Some of the kids from church brought them by."

Dad smiled and latched his watch.

"They're a great group of kids," he said.

"They only show up when there's a crisis," I said.

Dad looked at me hard. "Do you have something against people caring about you?"

I didn't want to upset Dad. "No. I'm just tired. Sorry." It wasn't right to be so mean.

Dad laid back down on his bed. I decided to test the waters and see if I could talk about Sara with him. After all, he'd known for a while.

"And I'm having a hard time lately. Things haven't been going so well."

"With school?"

"No, not school," I said.

"What then?"

Why didn't he say it? I took a deep breath.

"With Sara. I saw her at the movies with her . . . friend. I talked to Dorothy."

"I see," he said. He did look a little pale, but nothing like the gray at the hospital.

"What do you think?"

"I need to know what to do . . . I don't know what to think about anything. Do you think there's something wrong with me?" I shocked myself saying that last part.

Dad didn't react, except his face tensed and the muscles in his jaw moved. He put his hands behind his head.

"No, there's nothing wrong with you. You and Sara have always been close. Unless there's something you haven't told me?" Dad lifted his head, looked at me straight in the eye, and seemed to hold his breath.

"No, no. Nothing like that." Dad settled back onto his pillow. "She wants me to be okay with her having a . . . girlfriend."

"Has she said that?"

"I guess not exactly. She's sorry for keeping this from me, though. She wants me to forgive that."

"I think you should—forgive her for that," Dad said. "I think that's the easy part."

"It doesn't seem like it," I said, although I was

beginning to see that maybe that was an issue I was simply hiding behind.

"But, Dad, I thought I knew Sara. I thought we were alike."

Dad closed his eyes for a minute and then stared at the ceiling. Maybe he didn't hear me. "I thought I knew her."

"I used to think I had all the answers, Amy," he said, "but if I've learned anything through these hellish months, it's that you can't judge what's truly on the inside of anybody else. You're a strong person and you know what's right for you. Use your heart, use your head, and pray for guidance. That's all you can do."

I used to pray every night. I even prayed the night after Mom's accident. But then my prayers all became the same. "Please bring my mom back. Please bring my mom back. Please bring my mom back." Sure I believed in miracles, but I had no faith this could really happen. Praying became the same as hitting my head against a brick wall.

"You need to go to school tomorrow," Dad said.

He was right.

"I feel terrible everyone knew but me."

"Sara didn't know what to do," he said. "I've been talking to her mother, and frankly, no one knew what to do. Sometimes there's no good way to deal with a difficult situation like this."

"What do you think about it . . . I mean Sara's actual relationship?" I asked.

"What do I think? I'm not very happy, for both your sakes," he said. "I can't condone what Sara's doing and I hope you won't either. I've always taught you that sexual relations outside of marriage are wrong."

I nodded. My head hurt a little. I wouldn't be reacting this way, though, if Sara was involved with a boy, would I? No. I would have expected that. I wouldn't feel so confused. This—this was something else entirely. This was something she hid from me, something that affected our relationship. How was I supposed to act around her?

I said the only thing I was sure of. "Nothing changes how much Sara means to me."

"Let's hope this is just a phase. Sara's always been one to try new things, to push the envelope."

A phase. I didn't think it was, but didn't say so. It wasn't like Sara not to know what she wanted.

"But one thing I know is that her first concern was for you. Sara's been a true friend. There aren't many people in life you can count as true friends," he said. "She's been there for you when I haven't."

That was true. Sara had been there for me, and not just when there's been a crisis. In fact, it would have been a whole lot easier for her to just stay away this time. I would have made it easy on her.

I called Sara's house and got the answering machine.

"Sara," I said. "It's me. I just wanted to hear your voice. . . . I'll see you at school tomorrow. Meet me on the corner?" I hung up the phone.

Chapter 22

SARA WAITED ON THE CORNER, even though I was a bit early, then ran up to me, and nearly jumped on me to give me a big hug. A burden seemed to come off my shoulders and I hugged her back, although her words about propping me up still bothered me and I was hyperaware of the physical contact between us, even though it was just a hug. And I still didn't know how to handle her relationship with Anita.

"Amy, we're going to be okay," Sara said. "You'll see."

And I hoped maybe we were.

During the day, the whispering when I went by and the talking and speculating seemed to die down, or maybe it was just that I didn't care so much this time. It felt almost like a normal day.

Sara and I stayed late after school one day to help Ms. Newman with some work. Peter promised to meet me afterward so we could talk. The work took longer than I thought, and Sara said she'd finish so I could meet Peter on time. I went out into the hall and stopped to get a drink. When I finished and turned around, I saw Anita at the end of the hall with some of the other cheerleaders. Apparently, she was still on the squad. There had been rumors that she'd be kicked off. My feet took on a life of their own, and I started walking toward her. She looked up at me.

"Hi," I said. "Uh . . . How's it going?" What do you say to your best friend's girlfriend?

"Good, thanks," she said. I looked at my feet. Strange that this girl knew Sara maybe better than I did, and I couldn't think of a thing to say to her. So she talked instead.

"Now that you know about me and Sara," she said, "I'd appreciate it if you would back off a bit." Her words felt like a punch.

"What are you talking about?" I managed.

"Sara loves me, but she feels obligated to spend all her time worrying about you and checking on you and making sure you don't feel left out. Frankly, it's a real pain." She flipped her long hair behind her shoulder. "If you care about her, you've got to give her some space. Do you see what I'm saying?"

"Sara told you this?"

The other cheerleaders pretended to be busy stuffing their things into duffel bags.

"Look, Amy, it's obvious to everyone that you're becoming a real drain on Sara. Don't you want her to be happy? I thought I ought to say something."

I turned away, shocked, and walked almost smack into Peter. He glared at Anita and then followed me toward the door where I was walking fast. The cold November air stung my cheeks. The heavy scent of impending snow hung down over the trees like a fog.

Peter caught up to me. He was breathing hard.

"Hey, Amy. You all right?" he asked between gulps of air.

"What do you think?" I said, walking quickly.

"You know Sara never said those things. Anita doesn't know what she's talking about," he said, barely keeping up.

"Maybe she's right. Maybe all I've been is a big charity project. That's all I am to anybody." I was too angry to cry, so I ran instead, leaving Peter behind.

"Amy! Don't go!" Peter shouted, sounding almost angry.

"Why not?" I said, barely stopping as I turned to face him. I kept walking, backwards.

His face looked flushed and serious. "Because I care about you. . . . I love you." He stopped, exasperated, shook his head, and walked away from me.

Peter's words slowed me down, but he was gone before I thought to follow him. I didn't want to go home, so I started running again, and ran until my throat and lungs stung, and my legs felt wobbly. Then I walked. I wanted to be angry, I wanted to be hurt. But I was so tired. Exhausted. Exhausted from anger, exhausted from the hurt that ate away at my insides. Just exhausted from it all. The world seemed to be moving forward without me. I wouldn't pray for my mother to come back anymore. I wouldn't be angry she left me. I'd pray for peace and healing. I let go. And I prayed, harder than I'd ever prayed in my whole life. It was time to move forward.

Maybe Anita was right. Sara'd been *my* best friend, but what had I been to her?

I thought of Sara's stinging words to me. She'd been brave to say the truth. I needed to live, to breathe, independent of Sara.

I stayed out until I got stiff from the cold. There was that barely recognizable light feeling in my body again. When I got home, I shut the door behind me and tried to digest Peter's words.

Something smelled really, really good and it came from our kitchen. I heard my dad talking to someone and then Mrs. Bird from church came down the hall, slipping her arms into her coat.

"Amy, dear!" She nearly tripped over herself. She pinched my cheek like I was two years old. Dad followed behind her. He looked like himself again, and happier.

"Mrs. Bird and some other women from church made us a wonderful dinner," Dad said, his eyes lit up.

"Why?" It came out of my mouth before I realized how rude it sounded. Duh, she knew about Dad's illness.

My dad's face dropped, but Mrs. Bird didn't hesitate. "No reason except we thought you might enjoy it," she said. Then she leaned in close to my face and surprised me. "When I lost my husband, the hard part was later on, after everyone else had forgotten. It's been a year since your mom died. But I know you still need people to remember." She leaned in even farther. "And since your dad's illness . . . well, everyone needs a nice, hot, home-cooked meal once in a while."

The doorbell rang before I could even say "Thank you." And I meant it.

Dad opened the door while Mrs. Bird pinched my cheek again. I grabbed her arm and squeezed it and mouthed my thanks since no words came out when I saw Peter walk in. He shook Dad's hand.

"Come on in and eat with us," Dad said excitedly. "There's enough to feed an army here." For a moment I understood the connection between Dad and his work in the church and why he did it. All of a sudden, I missed it. I'd been missing it all this time.

When Dad disappeared into the kitchen, Peter put his arms around me.

"You don't give up, do you?" I said.

"Do you want me to?"

I touched the hair that hung in his face and brushed it back, and then I kissed him full on the lips, not caring whether Dad would see or not. Peter pulled me away from him after a minute and grinned. I was about to burst from the mixture of emotions. Houdini saved me by trying to climb up the leg of my jeans. I detached his claws from the fabric and held him against me and scratched his ears.

"Come on and eat while it's hot!" Dad yelled.

"It smells good," Peter said.

"It sure does," I said, though I hadn't the foggiest idea how I would manage to eat anything.

Chapter 23

THE WARMTH FROM MY MOTHER'S VOICE in my dream one night dissipated in the cold air of my room when I woke. Now that I had stopped wishing her back, I felt her more often. I could tell it had snowed without looking out the window because of the quality of light and shadows on my walls and the stillness of the dried leaves on the trees outside that normally rustled together. November. Had November always seemed like the longest month with the longest nights?

I felt vaguely confused and sad, but I felt a kind of peace with Peter and Dad and I was working on rejoining my old life somehow, minus Sara. I'd pretty much avoided her, unsure of my feelings. I wanted to be honest with her, but I couldn't be, yet, until I figured out how I felt. Cutting out Sara left a gaping hole, and I craved her presence in the long afternoons and evenings. The exhaustion of all the months between Novembers weighed heavy on me still, but at least it was something different from the pain. The stillness of the air and blue-black shadows lulled me back into a light sleep and into my dream where it left off, walking out of the store, our arms empty.

Someone pounded on my window. I grabbed the blanket and leaped into the farthest corner of my room when I saw the distorted face. My heart leaped to my mouth. The face pulled back and it was Sara. I threw the blanket toward the window, but it didn't go far because I was sitting on part of it. Sara was laughing and making smashed faces on the window.

I opened the window, my legs still shaky from being frightened. I flicked on the light and Sara covered her eyes. It had been a long time since my window was open and there were lots of dead flies in the window well. I blew them out, a few hitting Sara on the head and chest. The window only opened about two feet so I had to bend over to talk.

"You scared me to death. What are you doing?" I asked. She was wearing waders and had her hair tied back with fishing line. She stood on the wobbly wood ladder from her garage.

"I'm here to elope with you," she said, picking a dead fly out of her bangs. That was Sara, bold as ever, but her eyes quivered just a bit, and she didn't quite meet my eyes.

"Not funny," I said, and started to close the window. I was a little angry. I wasn't ready for this.

"Hang on, Amy." She grabbed the edge of the window to stop me from shutting it and lost her balance. I grabbed her arm to keep her from falling, but I couldn't grip the slick fabric of her jacket. The old ladder folded shut and she fell backward onto the grass, the ladder right on top of her.

"Sara?"

I heard her cursing under her breath, so I knew she wasn't dead. When she threw the ladder off and gave it a kick I shut the window, went downstairs, and out the back door.

"Be careful what you say. This is the pastor's house, you know. You can't just say anything you want around here," I said, only halfway joking. It had scared me when she fell, and I didn't need any more scares. Wouldn't it be easier just to let things be for now?

I guess I hurt her feelings, because she looked down and was quiet for a long time. Finally she put her hands on her hips, looked up at the sky, and took a deep breath.

"Look, Amy, it's a perfect morning for frogging." There was an inch of snow on the ground, the sky was clear, and it was cold. We'd never been in November before. Didn't frogs hibernate?

"I just thought you might want to go. We could use those flies you pelted me with for bait." She was trying to be her old self, but there was that scared look in her eyes.

"I don't know. My dad will be up soon and I didn't get much sleep . . . ," I began, not knowing what I wanted to say.

"Please, Amy." She stood there with a big hole ripped in her waders down the side of her right calf, a gash starting to ooze blood just above her ankle. The other pair of waders, a roll of fishing line, an extra hat, and our white frosting bucket were at her feet. My resolve faded. Man did I miss her.

"All right," I said. "But stash that ladder some-where so my dad doesn't see it. I'm going in to get dressed and get you a bandage for your leg. You're bleeding."

She didn't even look down at her leg, though the blood was running in rivulets down her ankle.

After we patched up Sara's leg and closed the hole in her waders with duct tape, we walked slowly toward the pond, our footsteps silent in the powdery snow. My mind asked why I was doing this, but my heart felt right, being with Sara the way we used to.

"I had a fight with Anita," Sara said. "We're taking a break from each other."

I stopped. This didn't affect me as much as I'd imagined it might. This wasn't about Anita. It was about me and Sara. Anita didn't make a difference one way or another. I started walking again.

"Peter told me what she said to you."

Peter. I could feel his warm lips on mine and his hair brushing against my face. My stomach flipped around.

"It's not true," she said. "None of it is true. I mean, the part about me worrying about you certainly is, but none of the rest of it. I don't know where she came up with that stuff."

My conversation with Anita felt forever ago. My feet moved forward, detached from my body. I savored the snow, the silence, and the cold air on my face. I thought about how Sandra was there only when I had a crisis. But how Sara had been constant. And how it would have been easier for her to stay away. And then, when she'd needed me, I'd avoided her, only thinking about my own problems. My face flushed hot despite the cold air.

She stopped and grabbed my arm. "Do you hear what I'm saying, Amy? None of what Anita said is true. You're my best friend and I would never give that up. For anything."

"I'm sorry," I said.

"Sorry about what?"

"Sorry that things have been . . . are . . . hard for you and I haven't helped you at all." I felt ashamed for how selfish I'd been.

"It has been hard," Sara said, real soft.

"But Anita was there for you, right?"

"She was part of the problem. I could have kept a better secret if I hadn't fallen for her."

"Did you break up with her just because she was mean to me?" I asked.

"Would you give me up for Peter?"

"No!" I said, before I even thought about it.

"You see?" she said, smiling. "Everything is the same between you and me. It always will be the same."

A car drove by and we were silent until it turned the corner.

"I'm going back to church," I said. "Like I used to. And the church . . . my beliefs . . . I love you, Sara, but I don't like what you're doing." There. I'd said it. My words fell flat on the cold air and hung there.

"I've never judged you for *your* beliefs, Amy. But that didn't stop me from being your best friend."

I hadn't thought of it this way. All those prayer meetings and Bible classes and my mom singing hymns all the time and my dad being a pastor. Some of it must have been hard for Sara to swallow.

I finally said, "It's just so complicated."

"We'll get through it," she said, and sighed.

"As long as there are no more secrets," I said.

"No more secrets."

"Promise?"

"Promise."

"I won't believe you without the code."

She laughed. "Walla Walla, Yakima, onions and cherries, sis boom ba!" The snap was loud and clear and stung our frozen fingers.

Chapter 24

"**W**HAT'S THIS?" Sara picked up part of the "Do Not Enter" yellow tape wrapped around the trees right before the forest gave way to the fenced area. We stepped over it and stopped past the trees, where the pond used to come into view. The fence had been partially pulled down and dragged away. Several large tractors were parked where the pond should be.

"The water's gone," I said. "They've drained the water." The words came out in steam puffs and disappeared above my head.

We stood there staring, the bucket hanging from our two hands in between us, still swinging from our abrupt stop.

Sara took a deep breath and ran forward, stopping by a bulldozer. She looked down at her feet and then knelt down in the shallow snow. Her hands moved in circles, brushing snow away from the ground. Finally she leaned forward on her arms, as if she were testing to see if the water hid underneath. I turned the bucket over and sat down, looking out over the expanding fields. The trees on the other side had been cleared, and I wondered what this place would look like in full sunlight, unhampered by shadows. Like any other athletic field, I decided.

When Sara came back, her knees and hands were muddy.

"It's really gone," she said.

I nodded my head and scooted over to one edge of the bucket. She sat on the other side, so we were back to back, the only way we fit. We sat together this way until the first trace of daylight made the snow shimmer in pockets on the mud field.

"You think we ought to find another place?" Sara whispered.

"No," I said. "No."

"It feels like we've lost something. Something more important than frogs," she said.

"What could be more important than frogs?" I said, and felt like laughing in spite of the sadness.

"You're right," she said. "The frogs are everything."

Our feet were numb and our cheeks red and chapped, but we sat, unmoving, on the old frosting bucket with our backs pressed together until the daylight erased all the shadows.